Marx Machiavelli Chesterton Emerson Joyce
Abbott Hardy Montaigne Cooper Austen
Defoe Melville Haggard Hugo
Christie Eliot Grimm
Stoker Carroll Molière
Wilde Maupassant Byron
Engels Schiller
Garnett Einstein Fitzgerald Smith
Goethe Hawthorne Kafka
Cotton Dostoyevsky Hall
Baum Kipling Doyle Willis
Leslie Dumas Henry Nietzsche
Flaubert Turgenev Balzac
Stockton Vatsyayana Crane
Burroughs Whitman Verne
Curtis Tocqueville Gogol Vinci
Homer Widger Tolstoy Busch
Darwin Thoreau
Potter Freud Zola Twain Plato Scott
Lawrence
Kant Jowett Stevenson Dickens
Andersen Cervantes Burton Hesse Harte
London Descartes
Poe Aristotle Wells Voltaire
Hale James Hastings Cooke
Bunner Shakespeare
Richter Chambers Irving
Doré Swift Dante Chekhov da Shaw Wodehouse Benedict Alcott
Pushkin
Newton

tredition®

tredition was established in 2006 by Sandra Latusseck and Soenke Schulz. Based in Hamburg, Germany, tredition offers publishing solutions to authors and publishing houses, combined with worldwide distribution of printed and digital book content. tredition is uniquely positioned to enable authors and publishing houses to create books on their own terms and without conventional manufacturing risks.

For more information please visit: www.tredition.com

TREDITION CLASSICS

This book is part of the TREDITION CLASSICS series. The creators of this series are united by passion for literature and driven by the intention of making all public domain books available in printed format again - worldwide. Most TREDITION CLASSICS titles have been out of print and off the bookstore shelves for decades. At tredition we believe that a great book never goes out of style and that its value is eternal. Several mostly non-profit literature projects provide content to tredition. To support their good work, tredition donates a portion of the proceeds from each sold copy. As a reader of a TREDITION CLASSICS book, you support our mission to save many of the amazing works of world literature from oblivion. See all available books at www.tredition.com.

Project Gutenberg

The content for this book has been graciously provided by Project Gutenberg. Project Gutenberg is a non-profit organization founded by Michael Hart in 1971 at the University of Illinois. The mission of Project Gutenberg is simple: To encourage the creation and distribution of eBooks. Project Gutenberg is the first and largest collection of public domain eBooks.

My Novel

Volume 5

Baron Edward Bulwer Lytton Lytton

Imprint

This book is part of TREDITION CLASSICS

Author: Baron Edward Bulwer Lytton Lytton
Cover design: Buchgut, Berlin – Germany

Publisher: tredition GmbH, Hamburg - Germany
ISBN: 978-3-8424-3135-5

www.tredition.com
www.tredition.de

BOOK FIFTH.

INITIAL CHAPTER.

CONTAINING MR. CAXTON's UNAVAILING CAUTION NOT TO BE DULL.

"I hope, Pisistratus," said my father, "that you do not intend to be dull?"

"Heaven forbid, sir! What could make you ask such a question? Intend!
No! if I am dull it is from innocence."

"A very long discourse upon knowledge!" said my father; "very long!
I should cut it out."

I looked upon my father as a Byzantian sage might have looked on a
Vandal. "Cut it out!"

"Stops the action, sir!" said my father, dogmatically.

"Action! But a novel is not a drama."

"No; it is a great deal longer,—twenty times as long, I dare say," replied Mr. Caxton, with a sigh.

"Well, sir, well! I think my Discourse upon Knowledge has much to do with the subject, is vitally essential to the subject; does not stop the action,—only explains and elucidates the action. And I am astonished, sir, that you, a scholar, and a cultivator of knowledge—"

"There, there!" cried my father, deprecatingly. "I yield, I yield! What better could I expect when I set up for a critic? What author ever lived that did not fly into a passion, even with his own father, if his father presumed to say, 'Cut out'!"

MRS. CAXTON.—"My dear Austin, I am sure Pisistratus did not mean to offend you, and I have no doubt he will take your—"

PISISTRATUS (hastily).—"Advice for the future, certainly. I will quicken the action, and—"

"Go on with the Novel," whispered Roland, looking up from his eternal account-book. "We have lost L200 by our barley!"

Therewith I plunged my pen into the ink, and my thoughts into the "Fair Shadowland."

CHAPTER II.

"HALT, cried a voice; and not a little surprised was Leonard when the stranger who had accosted him the preceding evening got into the chaise.

"Well," said Richard, "I am not the sort of man you expected, eh? Take time to recover yourself." And with these words Richard drew forth a book from his pocket, threw himself back, and began to read. Leonard stole many a glance at the acute, hardy, handsome face of his companion, and gradually recognized a family likeness to poor John, in whom, despite age and infirmity, the traces of no common share of physical beauty were still evident. And, with that quick link in ideas which mathematical aptitude bestows, the young student at once conjectured that he saw before him his uncle Richard. He had the discretion, however, to leave that gentleman free to choose his own time for introducing himself, and silently revolved the new thoughts produced by the novelty of his situation. Mr. Richard read with notable quickness,—sometimes cutting the leaves of the book with his penknife, sometimes tearing them open with his forefinger, sometimes skipping whole pages altogether. Thus he galloped to the end of the volume, flung it aside, lighted his cigar, and began to talk. He put many questions to Leonard relative to his rearing, and especially to the mode by which he had acquired his education; and Leonard, confirmed in the idea that he was replying to a kinsman, answered frankly.

Richard did not think it strange that Leonard should have acquired so much instruction with so little direct tuition. Richard Avenel himself had been tutor to himself. He had lived too long with our go-ahead brethren who stride the world on the other side the Atlantic with the seven-leagued boots of the Giant-killer, not to have caught their glorious fever for reading. But it was for a reading wholly different from that which was familiar to Leonard. The books he read must be new; to read old books would have seemed to him going back in the world. He fancied that new books necessarily contained new ideas,—a common mistake,—and our lucky adventurer was the man of his day.

Tired with talking, he at length chucked the book he had run through to Leonard, and taking out a pocket-book and pencil, amused himself with calculations on some detail of his business, after which he fell into an absorbed train of thought, part pecuniary, part ambitious.

Leonard found the book interesting: it was one of the numerous works, half-statistic, half-declamatory, relating to the condition of the working classes, which peculiarly distinguish our century, and ought to bind together rich and poor, by proving the grave attention which modern society bestows upon all that can affect the welfare of the last.

"Dull stuff! theory! claptrap!" said Richard, rousing himself from his revery at last; "it can't interest you."

"All books interest me, I think," said Leonard, "and this especially; for it relates to the working class, and I am one of them."

"You were yesterday, but you mayn't be to-morrow," answered Richard, good-humouredly, and patting him on the shoulder. "You see, my lad, that it is the middle class which ought to govern the country. What the book says about the ignorance of country magistrates is very good; but the man writes pretty considerable trash when he wants to regulate the number of hours a free-born boy should work at a factory,—only ten hours a day— pooh! and so lose two hours to the nation! Labour is wealth; and if we could get men to work twenty-four hours a day, we should be just twice as rich. If the march of civilization is to proceed," continued Richard, loftily, "men, and boys too, must not lie a bed doing nothing, all night, sir." Then, with a complacent tone, "We shall get to the twenty-four hours at last; and, by gad, we must, or we sha'n't flog the Europeans as we do now."

On arriving at the inn at which Richard had first made acquaintance with Mr. Dale, the coach by which he had intended to perform the rest of the journey was found to be full. Richard continued to perform the journey in postchaises, not without some grumbling at the expense, and incessant orders to the post-boys to make the best of the way. "Slow country this in spite of all its brag," said he,—"very slow. Time is money—they know that in the States; for why? they are all men of business there. Always slow in a country where a parcel of lazy, idle lords and dukes and baronets seem to think 'time is pleasure.'"

Towards evening the chaise approached the confines of a very large town, and Richard began to grow fidgety. His easy, cavalier air was abandoned. He withdrew his legs from the window, out of which they had been luxuriously dangling, pulled down his waistcoat, buckled more tightly his stock; it was clear that he was resuming the decorous dignity that belongs to state. He was like a monarch who, after travelling happy and incognito, returns to his capital. Leonard divined at once that they were nearing their journey's end.

Humble foot-passengers now looked at the chaise, and touched their hats. Richard returned the salutation with a nod,—a nod less gracious than condescending. The chaise turned rapidly to the left, and stopped before a small lodge, very new, very white, adorned with two Doric columns in stucco, and flanked by a large pair of gates. "Hollo!" cried the post- boy, and cracked his whip.

Two children were playing before the lodge, and some clothes were hanging out to dry on the shrubs and pales round the neat little building.

"Hang those brats! they are actually playing," growled Dick. "As I live, the jade has been washing again! Stop, boy!" During this soliloquy, a good-looking young woman had rushed from the door, slapped the children as, catching sight of the chaise, they ran towards the house, opened the gates, and dropping a courtesy to the ground, seemed to wish that she could drop into it altogether; so frightened and so trembling seemed she to shrink from the wrathful face which the master now put out of the window.

"Did I tell you, or did I not," said Dick, "that I would not have those horrid, disreputable cubs of yours playing just before my lodge gates?"

"Please, sir—"

"Don't answer me. And did I tell you, or did I not, that the next time I saw you making a drying-ground of my lilacs, you should go out, neck and crop—"

"Oh, please, sir—"

"You leave my lodge next Saturday! drive on, boy. The ingratitude and insolence of those common people are disgraceful to human nature," muttered Richard, with an accent of the bitterest misanthropy.

The chaise wheeled along the smoothest and freshest of gravel roads, and through fields of the finest land, in the highest state of cultivation. Rapid as was Leonard's survey, his rural eye detected the signs of a master in the art agronomial. Hitherto he had considered the squire's model farm as the nearest approach to good husbandry he had seen; for Jackeymo's finer skill was developed rather on the minute scale of market-gardening than what can fairly be called husbandry. But the squire's farm was degraded by many old-fashioned notions, and concessions to the whim of the eye, which would not be found in model farms nowadays,—large tangled hedgerows, which, though they constitute one of the beauties most picturesque in old England, make sad deductions from produce; great trees, overshadowing the corn and harbouring the birds; little patches of rough sward left to waste; and angles of woodland running into fields, exposing them to rabbits and blocking out the sun. These and such like blots on a gentleman-farmer's agriculture, common- sense and Giacomo had made clear to the acute comprehension of Leonard. No such faults were perceptible in Richard Avenel's domain. The fields lay in broad divisions, the hedges were clipped and narrowed into their proper destination of mere boundaries. Not a blade of wheat withered under the cold shade of a tree; not a yard of land lay waste; not a weed was to be seen, not a thistle to waft its baleful seed through the air: some young plantations were placed, not where the artist would put them, but just where the farmer wanted a fence from the wind. Was there no beauty in this? Yes, there was beauty of its kind,—beauty at once recognizable to the initiated, beauty of use and profit, beauty that could bear a monstrous high rent. And Leonard uttered a cry of admiration which thrilled through the heart of Richard Avenel.

"This IS farming!" said the villager.

"Well, I guess it is," answered Richard, all his ill-humour vanishing. "You should have seen the land when I bought it. But we new men, as they call us (damn their impertinence!) are the new blood of this country."

Richard Avenel never said anything more true. Long may the new blood circulate through the veins of the mighty giantess; but let the grand heart be the same as it has beat for proud ages.

The chaise now passed through a pretty shrubbery, and the house came into gradual view,—a house with a portico, all the offices carefully thrust out of sight.

The postboy dismounted and rang the bell.

"I almost think they are going to keep me waiting," said Mr. Richard, well-nigh in the very words of Louis XIV. But the fear was not realized,—the door opened; a well-fed servant out of livery presented himself. There was no hearty welcoming smile on his face, but he opened the chaise-door with demure and taciturn respect.

"Where's George? Why does he not come to the door?" asked Richard; descending from the chaise slowly, and leaning on the servant's outstretched arm with as much precaution as if he had had the gout.

Fortunately, George here came into sight, settling himself hastily into his livery coat.

"See to the things, both of you," said Richard, as he paid the postboy.

Leonard stood on the gravel sweep, gazing at the square white house.

"Handsome elevation—classical, I take it, eh?" said Richard, joining him. "But you should see the offices." He then, with familiar kindness, took Leonard by the arm, and drew him within. He showed him the hall, with a carved mahogany stand for hats; he showed him the drawing-room, and pointed out all its beauties; though it was summer, the drawing-room looked cold, as will look rooms newly furnished, with walls newly papered, in houses newly built. The furniture was handsome, and suited to the rank of a rich trader. There was no pretence about it, and therefore no vulgarity, which is more than can be said for the houses of many an Honourable Mrs. Somebody in Mayfair, with rooms twelve feet square, ebokeful of buhl, that would have had its proper place in the Tuileries. Then Richard showed him the library, with mahogany bookcases, and plate glass, and the fashionable authors handsomely bound. Your new men are much better friends to living authors than your old families who live in the country, and at most subscribe to a book-club. Then Richard took him up-stairs, and led him through the bedrooms,—all very clean and comfortable, and with every modern convenience; and pausing in a very pretty single gentleman's chamber, said, "This is your den. And now, can you guess who I am?"

"No one but my uncle Richard could be so kind," answered Leonard.

But the compliment did not flatter Richard. He was extremely disconcerted and disappointed. He had hoped that he should be taken for a lord at least, forgetful of all that he had said in disparagement of lords.

"Fish!" said he at last, biting his lip, "so you don't think that I look like a gentleman? Come, now, speak honestly."

Leonard, wonderingly, saw he had given pain, and with the good breeding which comes instinctively from good nature, replied, "I judge you by your heart, sir, and your likeness to my grandfather,—otherwise I should never have presumed to fancy we could be relations."

"Hum!" answered Richard. "You can just wash your hands, and then come down to dinner; you will hear the gong in ten ininutes. There's the bell,—ring for what you want." With that, he turned on his heel; and descending the stairs, gave a look into the dining-room, and admired the plated salver on the sideboard, and the king's pattern spoons and silver on the table. Then he walked to the looking-glass over the mantelpiece; and, wishing to survey the whole effect of his form, mounted a chair. He was just getting into an attitude which he thought imposing, when the butler entered, and, being London bred, had the discretion to try to escape unseen;

but Richard caught sight of him in the looking-glass, and coloured up to the temples.

"Jarvis," said he, mildly, "Jarvis, put me in mind to have these inexpressibles altered."

CHAPTER III.

/A propos/ of the inexpressibles, Mr. Richard did not forget to provide his nephew with a much larger wardrobe than could have been thrust into Dr. Riccabocca's knapsack. There was a very good tailor in the town, and the clothes were very well made. And, but for an air more ingenuous, and a cheek that, despite study and night vigils, retained much of the sunburned bloom of the rustic, Leonard Fairfield might now have almost passed, without disparaging comment, by the bow-window at White's. Richard burst into an immoderate fit of laughter when he first saw the watch which the poor Italian had bestowed upon Leonard; but to atone for the laughter, he made him a present of a very pretty substitute, and bade him "lock up his turnip." Leonard was more hurt by the jeer at his old patron's gift than pleased by his uncle's. But Richard Avenel had no conception of sentiment. It was not for many days that Leonard could reconcile himself to his uncle's manner. Not that the peasant could pretend to judge of its mere conventional defects; but there is an ill breeding to which, whatever our rank and nurture, we are almost equally sensitive,—the ill breeding that comes from want of consideration for others. Now, the squire was as homely in his way as Richard Avenel, but the squire's bluntness rarely hurt the feelings; and when it did so, the squire perceived and hastened to repair his blunder. But Mr. Richard, whether kind or cross, was always wounding you in some little delicate fibre,—not from malice, but from the absence of any little delicate fibres of his own. He was really, in many respects, a most excellent man, and certainly a very valuable citizen—; but his merits wanted the fine tints and fluent curves that constitute beauty of character. He was honest, but sharp in his practice, and with a keen eye to his interests. He was just, but as a matter of business. He made no allowances, and did not leave to his justice the large margin of tenderness and mercy. He was generous, but rather from an idea of what was due to himself than with much thought of the pleasure he gave to others; and he even regarded generosity as a capital put out to interest. He expected a great deal of gratitude in return, and, when he obliged a man, considered that he had bought a slave. Every needy voter knew where to come, if he wanted relief or a loan; but woe to him if he had ventured to express hesitation when Mr. Avenel told him how he must vote.

In this town Richard had settled after his return from America, in which country he had enriched himself,—first, by spirit and industry, lastly, by bold speculation and good luck. He invested his fortune in business, —became a partner in a large brewery, soon bought out his associates, and then took a principal share in a flourishing corn-mill. He prospered rapidly,—bought a property of some two or three hundred acres, built a house, and resolved to enjoy himself, and make a figure. He had now become the leading man of the town, and the boast to Audley Egerton that he could return one of the members, perhaps both, was by no means an exaggerated estimate of his power. Nor was his proposition, according to his own views, so unprincipled as it appeared to the statesman. He had taken a great dislike to both the sitting members,—a dislike natural to a sensible man of moderate politics, who had something to lose. For Mr. Slappe, the active member, who was head-over-ears in debt, was one of the furious democrats—rare before the Reform Bill,—and whose opinions were held dangerous even by the mass of a Liberal constituency; while Mr. Sleekie, the gentleman member who laid by L5000 every year from his dividends in the Funds, was one of those men whom Richard justly pronounced to be "humbugs,"—men who curry favour with the extreme party by voting for measures sure not to be carried; while if there was the least probability of coming to a decision that would lower the money market. Mr. Sleekie was seized with a well-timed influenza. Those politicians are common enough now. Propose to march to the Millennium, and they are your men. Ask them to march a quarter of a mile, and they fall to feeling their pockets, and trembling for fear of the footpads. They are never so joyful as when there is no chance of a victory. Did they beat the minister, they would be carried out of the House in a fit.

Richard Avenel—despising both these gentlemen, and not taking kindly to the Whigs since the great Whig leaders were lords—had looked with a friendly eye to the government as it then existed, and especially to Audley Egerton, the enlightened representative of commerce. But in giving Audley and his colleagues the benefit of his influence, through conscience, he thought it all fair and right to have a quid pro quo, and, as he had so frankly confessed, it was his whim to rise up "Sir Richard." For this worthy citizen abused the aristocracy much on the same principle as the fair Olivia depreciated Squire Thornhill,—he had a sneaking affection for what he abused. The society of Screwstown was, like most provincial capitals, composed of two classes,—the commercial and the exclusive. These last dwelt chiefly apart, around the ruins of an old abbey; they affected its antiquity in their pedigrees, and had much of its ruin in their finances. Widows of rural thanes in the neighbourhood, genteel spinsters, officers retired on half-pay, younger sons of rich squires, who had now become old bachelors,—in short, a very respectable, proud, aristocratic set, who thought more of themselves than do all the Gowers and Howards, Courtenays and Seymours, put together. It had early been the ambition of Richard Avenel to be admitted into this sublime coterie; and, strange to say, he had partially succeeded. He was never more happy than when he was asked to their card-parties, and never more unhappy than when he was actually there. Various circumstances combined to raise Mr. Avenel into this elevated society. First, he was unmarried, still very handsome, and in that society there was a large proportion of unwedded females. Secondly, he was the only rich trader in Screwstown who kept a good cook, and professed to give dinners, and the half-pay captains and colonels swallowed the host for the sake of the venison. Thirdly, and principally, all these exclusives abhorred the two sitting members, and "idem nolle idem velle de republica, ea firma amicitia est;" that is, congeniality in politics pieces porcelain and crockery together better than the best diamond cement. The sturdy Richard Avenel, who valued himself on American independence, held these ladies and gentlemen in an awe that was truly Brahminical. Whether it was that, in England, all notions, even of liberty, are mixed up historically, traditionally, socially, with that fine and subtle element of aristocracy which, like the press, is the air we breathe; or whether Richard imagined that he really became magnetically imbued with the virtues of these silver pennies and gold seven-shilling pieces, distinct from the vulgar coinage in popular use, it is hard to say. But the truth must be told,—Richard Avenel was a notable tuft-hunter. He had a great longing to marry out of this society; but he had not yet seen any one sufficiently high-born and high-bred to satisfy his aspirations. In the meanwhile, he had convinced himself that his way would be smooth could he offer to make his ultimate choice "My Lady;" and he felt that it would be a proud hour in his life when he could walk before stiff Colonel Pompley to the sound of "Sir Richard." Still, however disappointed at the ill-success of his bluff diplomacy with Mr. Egerton, and however yet cherishing the most vindictive resentment against that individual, he did not, as many would have done, throw up his political convictions out of personal spite. He reserved his private grudge for some special occasion, and continued still to support the Administration, and to hate one of the ministers.

But, duly to appreciate the value of Richard Avenel, and in just counterpoise to all his foibles, one ought to have seen what he had effected for the town. Well might he boast of "new blood;" he had done as much for the town as he had for his fields. His energy, his quick comprehension of public utility, backed by his wealth and bold, bullying, imperious character, had sped the work of civilization as if with the celerity and force of a steam-engine.

If the town were so well paved and so well lighted, if half-a-dozen squalid lanes had been transformed into a stately street, if half the town no longer depended on tanks for their water, if the poor-rates were reduced one-third, praise to the brisk new blood which Richard Avenel had infused into vestry and corporation. And his example itself was so contagious!

"There was not a plate-glass window in the town when I came into it," said Richard Avenel; "and now look down the High Street!" He took the credit to himself, and justly; for though his own business did not require windows of plate-glass, he had awakened the spirit of enterprise which adorns a whole city.

Mr. Avenel did not present Leonard to his friends for more than a fortnight. He allowed him to wear off his rust. He then gave a grand dinner, at which his nephew was formally introduced, and, to his great wrath and disappointment, never opened his lips. How could he, poor youth, when Miss Clarina Mowbray only talked upon high life, till proud Colonel Pompley went in state through the history of the Siege of Seringapatam?

CHAPTER IV.

While Leonard accustoms himself gradually to the splendours that surround him, and often turns with a sigh to the remembrance of his mother's cottage and the sparkling fount in the Italian's flowery garden, we will make with thee, O reader, a rapid flight to the metropolis, and drop ourselves amidst the gay groups that loiter along the dusty ground or loll over the roadside palings of Hyde Park. The season is still at its height; but the short day of fashionable London life, which commences two hours after noon, is in its decline.

The crowd in Rotten Row begins to thin. Near the statue of Achilles, and apart from all other loungers, a gentleman, with one hand thrust into his waistcoat, and the other resting on his cane, gazed listlessly on the horsemen and carriages in the brilliant ring. He was still in the prime of life, at the age when man is usually the most social,—when the acquaintances of youth have ripened into friendships, and a personage of some rank and fortune has become a well-known feature in the mobile face of society. But though, when his contemporaries were boys scarce at college, this gentleman had blazed foremost amongst the princes of fashion, and though he had all the qualities of nature and circumstance which either retain fashion to the last, or exchange its false celebrity for a graver repute, he stood as a stranger in that throng of his countrymen. Beauties whirled by to the toilet, statesmen passed on to the senate, dandies took flight to the clubs; and neither nods, nor becks, nor wreathed smiles said to the solitary spectator, "Follow us,— thou art one of our set." Now and then some middle-aged beau, nearing the post of the loiterer, turned round to look again; but the second glance seemed to dissipate the recognition of the first, and the beau silently continued his way.

"By the tomb of my fathers!" said the solitary to himself, "I know now what a dead man might feel if he came to life again, and took a peep at the living."

Time passed on,—the evening shades descended fast. Our stranger in London had well-nigh the Park to himself. He seemed to breathe more freely as he saw that the space was so clear.

"There's oxygen in the atmosphere now," said he, half aloud; "and I can walk without breathing in the gaseous fumes of the multitude. Oh, those chemists—what dolts they are! They tell us that crowds taint the air, but they never guess why! Pah, it is not the lungs that poison the element,—it is the reek of bad hearts. When a periwigpated fellow breathes on me, I swallow a mouthful of care. Allons! my friend Nero; now for a stroll." He touched with his cane a large Newfoundland dog, who lay stretched near his feet, and dog and man went slow through the growing twilight, and over the brown dry turf. At length our solitary paused, and threw himself on a bench under a tree. "Half-past eight!" said he, looking at his watch, "one may smoke one's cigar without shocking the world."

He took out his cigar-case, struck a light, and in another moment reclined at length on the bench, seemed absorbed in regarding the smoke, that scarce coloured ere it vanished into air.

"It is the most barefaced lie in the world, my Nero," said he, addressing his dog, "this boasted liberty of man! Now, here am I, a free-born Englishman, a citizen of the world, caring—I often say to myself—caring not a jot for Kaiser or Mob; and yet I no more dare smoke this cigar in the Park at half-past six, when all the world is abroad, than I dare pick my Lord Chancellor's pocket, or hit the Archbishop of Canterbury a thump on the nose. Yet no law in England forbids me my cigar, Nero! What is law at half-past eight was not crime at six and a half! Britannia says, 'Man, thou art free, and she lies like a commonplace woman. O Nero, Nero! you enviable dog! you serve but from liking. No thought of the world costs you one wag of the tail. Your big heart and true instinct suffice you for reason and law. You would want nothing to your felicity, if in these moments of ennui you would but smoke a cigar. Try it, Nero! —try it!" And, rising from his incumbent posture, he sought to force the end of the weed between the teeth of the dog.

While thus gravely engaged, two figures had approached the place. The one was a man who seemed weak and sickly. His threadbare coat was buttoned to the chin, but hung large on his shrunken breast. The other was a girl, who might be from twelve to fourteen, on whose arm he leaned heavily. Her cheek was wan, and there was a patient, sad look on her face, which seemed so settled that you would think she could never have known the mirthfulness of childhood.

"Pray rest here, Papa," said the child, softly; and she pointed to the bench, without taking heed of its pre-occupant, who now, indeed, confined to one corner of the seat, was almost hidden by the shadow of the tree.

The man sat down, with a feeble sigh, and then, observing the stranger, raised his hat, and said, in that tone of voice which betrays the usages of polished society, "Forgive me if I intrude on you, sir."

The stranger looked up from his dog, and seeing that the girl was standing, rose at once, as if to make room for her on the bench.

But still the girl did not heed him. She hung over her father, and wiped his brow tenderly with a little kerchief which she took from her own neck for the purpose.

Nero, delighted to escape the cigar, had taken to some unwieldy curvets and gambols, to vent the excitement into which he had been thrown; and now returning, approached the bench with a low growl of surprise, and sniffed at the intruders of his master's privacy.

"Come here, sir," said the master. "You need not fear him," he added, addressing himself to the girl.

But the girl, without turning round to him, cried in a voice rather of anguish than alarm, "He has fainted! Father! Father!"

The stranger kicked aside his dog, which was in the way, and loosened the poor man's stiff military stock. While thus charitably engaged, the moon broke out, and the light fell full on the pale, careworn face of the unconscious sufferer.

"This face seems not unfamiliar to me, though sadly changed," said the stranger to himself; and bending towards the girl, who had sunk on her knees, and was chafing her father's hand, he asked, "My child, what is your father's name?"

The child continued her task, too absorbed to answer.

The stranger put his hand on her shoulder, and repeated the question.

"Digby," answered the child, almost unconsciously; and as she spoke the man's senses began to return. In a few minutes more he had sufficiently recovered to falter forth his thanks to the stranger. But the last took his hand, and said, in a voice at once tremulous and soothing, "Is it possible that I see once more an old brother in arms? Algernon Digby, I do not forget you; but it seems England has forgotten."

A hectic flush spread over the soldier's face, and he looked away from the speaker as he answered,—

"My name is Digby, it is true, sir; but I do not think we have met before. Come, Helen, I am well now,—we will go home."

"Try and play with that great dog, my child," said the stranger,—"I want to talk with your father."

The child bowed her submissive head, and moved away; but she did not play with the dog.

"I must reintroduce myself formally, I see," quoth the stranger. "You were in the same regiment with myself, and my name is L'E-strange."

"My Lord," said the soldier, rising, "forgive me that— "

"I don't think that it was the fashion to call me 'my lord' at the mess- table. Come, what has happened to you?—on half-pay?"

Mr. Digby shook his head mournfully.

"Digby, old fellow, can you lend me L100?" said Lord L'Estrange, clapping his ci-devant brother-officer on the shoulder, and in a tone of voice that seemed like a boy's, so impudent was it, and devil-me-Garish. "No! Well, that's lucky, for I can lend it to you." Mr. Digby burst into tears.

Lord L'Estrange did not seem to observe the emotion, but went on carelessly,—

"Perhaps you don't know that, besides being heir to a father who is not only very rich, but very liberal, I inherited, on coming of age, from a maternal relation, a fortune so large that it would bore me to death if I were obliged to live up to it. But in the days of our old acquaintance, I fear we were both sad extravagant fellows, and I dare say I borrowed of you pretty freely."

"Me! Oh, Lord L'Estrange!"

"You have married since then, and reformed, I suppose. Tell me, old friend, all about it."

Mr. Digby, who by this time had succeeded in restoring some calm to his shattered nerves, now rose, and said in brief sentences, but clear, firm tones,—

"My Lord, it is idle to talk of me,—useless to help me. I am fast dying. But my child there, my only child" (he paused for an instant, and went on rapidly). "I have relations in a distant county, if I could but get to them; I think they would, at least, provide for her. This has been for weeks my hope, my dream, my prayer. I cannot afford the journey except by your help. I have begged without shame for myself; shall I be ashamed, then, to beg for her?"

"Digby," said L'Estrange, with some grave alteration of manner, "talk neither of dying nor begging. You were nearer death when the balls whistled round you at Waterloo. If soldier meets soldier and says 'Friend, thy purse,' it is not begging, but brotherhood. Ashamed! By the soul of Belisarius! if I needed money, I would stand at a crossing with my Waterloo medal over my breast, and say to each sleek citizen I had helped to save from the sword of the Frenchman, 'It is your shame if I starve.' Now, lean upon me; I see you should be at home: which way?"

The poor soldier pointed his hand towards Oxford Street, and reluctantly accepted the proffered arm.

"And when you return from your relations, you will call on me? What— hesitate? Come, promise."

"I will."

"On your honour."

"If I live, on my honour."

"I am staying at present at Knightsbridge, with my father; but you will always hear of my address at No.—, Grosvenor Square, Mr. Egerton's. So you have a long journey before you?"

"Very long."

"Do not fatigue yourself,—travel slowly. Ho, you foolish child! I see you are jealous of me. Your father has another arm to spare you."

Thus talking, and getting but short answers, Lord L'Estrange continued to exhibit those whimsical peculiarities of character, which had obtained for him the repute of heartlessness in the world. Perhaps the reader may think the world was not in the right; but if ever the world does judge rightly of the character of a man who does not live for the world nor talk of the world nor feel with the world, it will be centuries after the soul of Harley L'Estrange has done with this planet.

CHAPTER V.

Lord L'Estrange parted company with Mr. Digby at the entrance of Oxford Street. The father and child there took a cabriolet. Mr. Digby directed the driver to go down the Edgware Road. He refused to tell L'Estrange his address, and this with such evident pain, from the sores of pride, that L'Estrange could not press the point. Reminding the soldier of his promise to call, Harley thrust a pocket-book into his hand, and walked off hastily towards Grosvenor Square.

He reached Audley Egerton's door just as that gentleman was getting out of his carriage; and the two friends entered the house together.

"Does the nation take a nap to-night?" asked L'Estrange. "Poor old lady! She hears so much of her affairs, that she may well boast of her constitution: it must be of iron."

"The House is still sitting," answered Audley, seriously, and with small heed of his friend's witticism. "But it is not a Government motion, and the division will be late, so I came home; and if I had not found you here, I should have gone into the Park to look for you."

"Yes; one always knows where to find me at this hour, nine o'clock P.M., cigar, Hyde Park. There is not a man in England so regular in his habits."

Here the friends reached a drawing-room in which the member of parliament seldom sat, for his private apartments were all on the ground-floor.

"But it is the strangest whim of yours, Harley," said he.

"What?"

To affect detestation of ground-floors."

"Affect! O sophisticated man, of the earth, earthy! Affect!—nothing less natural to the human soul than a ground-floor. We are quite far enough from Heaven, mount as many stairs as we will, without grovelling by preference."

"According to that symbolical view of the case," said Audley, "you should lodge in an attic."

"So I would, but that I abhor new slippers. As for hairbrushes, I am indifferent."

"What have slippers and hair-brushes to do with attics?"

"Try! Make your bed in an attic, and the next morning you will have neither slippers nor hair-brushes!"

"What shall I have done with them?"

"Shied them at the cats!"

"What odd things you say, Harley!"

"Odd! By Apollo and his nine spinsters! there is no human being who has so little imagination as a distinguished member of parliament. Answer me this, thou solemn Right Honourable,—Hast thou climbed to the heights of august contemplation? Hast thou gazed on the stars with the rapt eye of song? Hast thou dreamed of a love known to the angels, or sought to seize in the Infinite the mystery of life?"

"Not I indeed, my poor Harley."

"Then no wonder, poor Audley, that you cannot conjecture why he who makes his bed in an attic, disturbed by base catterwauls, shies his slippers at cats. Bring a chair into the balcony. Nero spoiled my cigar to-night. I am going to smoke now. You never smoke. You can look on the shrubs in the square."

Audley slightly shrugged his shoulders, but he followed his friend's counsel and example, and brought his chair into the balcony. Nero came too, but at sight and smell of the cigar prudently retreated, and took refuge under the table.

"Audley Egerton, I want something from Government."

"I am delighted to hear it."

"There was a cornet in my regiment, who would have done better not to have come into it. We were, for the most part of us, puppies and fops."

"You all fought well, however."

"Puppies and fops do fight well. Vanity and valour generally go together. CAesar, who scratched his head with due care of his scanty curls, and even in dying thought of the folds in his toga; Walter Raleigh, who could not walk twenty yards because of the gems in his shoes; Alcibiades, who lounged into the Agora with doves in his bosom, and an apple in his hand; Murat, bedizened in gold lace and furs; and Demetrius, the City-Taker, who made himself up like a French marquise, were all pretty good fellows at fighting. A slovenly hero like Cromwell is a paradox in nature, and a marvel in history. But to return to my cornet. We were rich; he was poor. When the pot of clay swims down the stream with the brass-pots, it is sure of a smash. Men said Digby was stingy; I saw he was extravagant. But every one, I fear, would be rather thought stingy than poor. /Bref/ —I left the army, and saw him no more till to-night. There was never shabby poor gentleman on the stage more awfully shabby, more pathetically gentleman. But, look ye, this man has fought for England. It was no child's play at Waterloo, let me tell you, Mr. Egerton; and, but for such men, you would be at best a /sous prefet/, and your parliament a Provincial Assembly. You must do something for Digby. What shall it be?"

"Why, really, my dear Harley, this man was no great friend of yours, eh?"

"If he were, he would not want the Government to help him,—he would not be ashamed of taking money from me."

"That is all very fine, Harley; but there are so many poor officers, and so little to give. It is the most difficult thing in the world that which you ask me. Indeed, I know nothing can be done: he has his half- pay?"

"I think not; or, if he has it, no doubt it all goes on his debts.
That's nothing to us: the man and his child are starving."

"But if it is his own fault,—if he has been imprudent?"

"Ah, well, well; where the devil is Nero?"

"I am so sorry I can't oblige you. If it were anything else—"

"There is something else. My valet—I can't turn him adrift-excellent fellow, but gets drunk now and then. Will you find him a place in the Stamp Office?"

"With pleasure."

"No, now I think of it, the man knows my ways: I must keep him. But my old wine-merchant—civil man, never dunned—is a bankrupt. I am under great obligations to him, and he has a very pretty daughter. Do you think you could thrust him into some small place in the Colonies, or make him a King's Messenger, or something of the sort?"

"If you very much wish it, no doubt I can."

"My dear Audley, I am but feeling my way: the fact is, I want something for myself."

"Ah, that indeed gives me pleasure!" cried Egerton, with animation.

"The mission to Florence will soon be vacant,—I know it privately. The place would quite suit me. Pleasant city; the best figs in Italy; very little to do. You could sound Lord on the subject."

"I will answer beforehand. Lord—would be enchanted to secure to the public service a man so accomplished as yourself, and the son of a peer like Lord Lansmere."

Harley L'Estrange sprang to his feet, and flung his cigar in the face of a stately policeman who was looking up at the balcony.

"Infamous and bloodless official!" cried Harley L'Estrange; "so you could provide for a pimple-nosed lackey, for a wine-merchant who has been poisoning the king's subjects with white lead,—or sloe-juice,—for an idle sybarite, who would complain of a crumpled rose-leaf; and nothing, in all the vast patronage of England, for a broken-down soldier, whose dauntless breast was her rampart?"

"Harley," said the member of parliament, with his calm, sensible smile, "this would be a very good claptrap at a small theatre; but there is nothing in which parliament demands such rigid economy as the military branch of the public service; and no man for whom it is so hard to effect what we must plainly call a job as a subaltern officer who has done nothing more than his duty,—and all military men do that. Still, as you take it so earnestly, I will use what interest I can at the War Office, and get him, perhaps, the mastership of a barrack."

"You had better; for, if you do not, I swear I will turn Radical, and come down to your own city to oppose you, with Hunt and Cobbett to canvass for me."

"I should be very glad to see you come into parliament, even as a Radical, and at my expense," said Audley, with great kindness; "but the air is growing cold, and you are not accustomed to our climate. Nay, if you are too poetic for catarrhs and rheums, I'm not,—come in."

CHAPTER VI.

Lord L'Estrange threw himself on a sofa, and leaned his cheek on his hand thoughtfully. Audley Egerton sat near him, with his arms folded, and gazed on his friend's face with a soft expression of aspect, which was very unusual to the firm outline of his handsome features. The two men were as dissimilar in person as the reader will have divined that they were in character. All about Egerton was so rigid, all about L'Estrange so easy. In every posture of Harley's there was the unconscious grace of a child. The very fashion of his garments showed his abhorrence of restraint. His clothes were wide and loose; his neckcloth, tied carelessly, left his throat half bare. You could see that he had lived much in warm and southern lands, and contracted a contempt for conventionalities; there was as little in his dress as in his talk of the formal precision of the North. He was three or four years younger than Audley, but he looked at least twelve years younger. In fact, he was one of those men to whom old age seems impossible; voice, look, figure, had all the charm of youth: and perhaps it was from this gracious youthfulness—at all events, it was characteristic of the kind of love he inspired—that neither his parents, nor the few friends admitted into his intimacy, ever called him, in their habitual intercourse, by the name of his title. He was not L'Estrange with them, he was Harley; and by that familiar baptismal I will usually designate him. He was not one of those men whom author or reader wish to view at a distance, and remember as "my Lord"—it was so rarely that he remembered it himself. For the rest, it had been said of him by a shrewd wit, "He is so natural that every one calls him affected." Harley L'Estrange was not so critically handsome as Audley Egerton; to a commonplace observer, he was only rather good- looking than otherwise. But women said that he had "a beautiful countenance," and they were not wrong. He wore his hair, which was of a fair chestnut, long, and in loose curls; and instead of the Englishman's whiskers, indulged in the foreigner's mustache. His complexion was delicate, though not effeminate: it was rather the delicacy of a student than of a woman. But in his clear gray eye there was a wonderful vigour of life. A skilful physiologist, looking only into that eye, would have recognized rare stamina of constitution,—a nature so rich that, while easily disturbed, it would require all the effects of time, or all the fell combinations of passion and grief, to exhaust it. Even now, though so thoughtful, and even so sad, the rays of that eye were as concentrated and steadfast as the light of the diamond.

"You were only, then, in jest," said Audley, after a long silence, "when you spoke of this mission to Florence. You have still no idea of entering into public life?"

"None."

"I had hoped better things when I got your promise to pass one season in London; but, indeed, you have kept your promise to the ear to break it to the spirit. I could not presuppose that you would shun all society, and be as much of a hermit here as under the vines of Como."

"I have sat in the Strangers' Gallery, and heard your great speakers; I have been in the pit of the opera, and seen your fine ladies; I have walked your streets; I have lounged in your parks, and I say that I can't fall in love with a faded dowager, because she fills up her wrinkles with rouge."

"Of what dowager do you speak?" asked the matter-of-fact Audley.

"She has a great many titles. Some people call her Fashion, you busy men, Politics: it is all one,—tricked out and artificial. I mean London Life. No, I can't fall in love with her, fawning old harridan!"

"I wish you could fall in love with something." "I wish I could, with all my heart."

"But you are so /blaze/."

"On the contrary, I am so fresh. Look out of the window—what do you see?"

"Nothing!"

"Nothing?"

"Nothing but houses and dusty lilacs, my coachman dozing on his box, and two women in pattens crossing the kennel."

"I see not those where I lie on the sofa. I see but the stars. And I feel for them as I did when I was a schoolboy at Eton. It is you who are /blaze/, not I. Enough of this. You do not forget my commission with respect to the exile who has married into your brother's family?"

"No; but here you set me a task more difficult than that of saddling your cornet on the War Office."

"I know it is difficult, for the counter influence is vigilant and strong; but, on the other hand, the enemy is so damnable a traitor that one must have the Fates and the household gods on one's side."

"Nevertheless," said the practical Audley, bending over a book on the table; "I think that the best plan would be to attempt a compromise with the traitor."

"To judge of others by myself," answered Harley, with spirit, "it were less bitter to put up with wrong than to palter with it for compensation. And such wrong! Compromise with the open foe—that maybe done with honour; but with the perjured friend—that were to forgive the perjury!"

"You are too vindictive," said Egerton; "there may be excuses for the friend, which palliate even— "

"Hush! Audley, hush! or I shall think the world has indeed corrupted you. Excuse for the friend who deceives, who betrays! No, such is the true outlaw of Humanity; and the Furies surround him even while he sleeps in the temple."

The man of the world lifted his eyes slowly on the animated face of one still natural enough for the passions. He then once more returned to his book, and said, after a pause, "It is time you should marry, Harley."

"No," answered L'Estrange, with a smile at this sudden turn in the conversation, "not time yet; for my chief objection to that change in life is, that the women nowadays are too old for me, or I am too young for them. A few, indeed, are so infantine that one is ashamed to be their toy; but most are so knowing that one is afraid to be their dupe. The first, if they condescend to love you, love you as the biggest doll they have yet dandled, and for a doll's good qualities,—your pretty blue eyes and your exquisite millinery. The last, if they prudently accept you, do so on algebraical principles; you are but the X or the Y that represents a certain aggregate of goods matrimonial,—pedigree, title, rent-roll, diamonds, pin-money, opera-box. They cast you up with the help of mamma, and you wake some morning to find that plus wife minus affection equals—the Devil!"

"Nonsense," said Audley, with his quiet, grave laugh. "I grant that it is often the misfortune of a man in your station to be married rather for what he has than for what he is; but you are tolerably penetrating, and not likely to be deceived in the character of the woman you court."

"Of the woman I court?—No! But of the woman I marry, very likely indeed! Woman is a changeable thing, as our Virgil informed us at school; but her change par excellence is from the fairy you woo to the brownie you wed. It is not that she has been a hypocrite,—it is that she is a transmigration. You marry a girl for her accomplishments. She paints charmingly, or plays like Saint Cecilia. Clap a ring on her finger, and she never draws again,—except perhaps your caricature on the back of a letter,—and never opens a piano after the honeymoon. You marry her for her sweet temper; and next year, her nerves are so shattered that you can't contradict her but you are whirled into a storm of hysterics. You marry her because she declares she hates balls and likes quiet; and ten to one but what she becomes a patroness at Almack's, or a lady-in-waiting."

"Yet most men marry, and most men survive the operation."

"If it were only necessary to live, that would be a consolatory and encouraging reflection. But to live with peace, to live with dignity, to live with freedom, to live in harmony with your thoughts, your habits, your aspirations—and this in the perpetual companionship of a person to whom you have given the power to wound your peace, to assail your dignity, to cripple your freedom, to jar on each thought and each habit, and bring you down to the meanest details of earth, when you invite her, poor soul, to soar to the spheres—that makes the To Be or Not To Be, which is the question."

"If I were you, Harley, I would do as I have heard the author of 'Sandford and Merton' did,—choose out a child and educate her yourself, after your own heart."

"You have hit it," answered Harley, seriously. "That has long been my idea,—a very vague one, I confess. But I fear I shall be an old man before I find even the child."

"Ah!" he continued, yet more earnestly, while the whole character of his varying countenance changed again,—"ah, if indeed I could discover what I seek,—one who, with the heart of a child, has the mind of a woman; one who beholds in nature the variety, the charm, the never feverish, ever healthful excitement that others vainly seek in the bastard sentimentalities of a life false with artificial forms; one who can comprehend, as by intuition, the rich poetry with which creation is clothed,—poetry so clear to the child when enraptured with the flower, or when wondering at the star! If on me such exquisite companionship were bestowed—why, then—" He paused, sighed deeply, and, covering his face with his hand, resumed, in faltering accents,—

"But once—but once only, did such vision of the Beautiful made Human rise before me,—rise amidst 'golden exhalations of the dawn.' It beggared my life in vanishing. You know only—you only—how—how—"

He bowed his head, and the tears forced themselves through his clenched fingers.

"So long ago!" said Audley, sharing his friend's emotion. "Years so long and so weary, yet still thus tenacious of a mere boyish memory!"

"Away with it, then!" cried Harley, springing to his feet, and with a laugh of strange merriment. "Your carriage still waits: set me home before you go to the House."

Then laying his hand lightly on his friend's shoulder, he said, "Is it for you, Audley Egerton, to speak sneeringly of boyish memories? What else is it that binds us together? What else warms my heart when I meet you? What else draws your thoughts from blue-books and beer-bills to waste them on a vagrant like me? Shake hands. Oh, friend of my boyhood! recollect the oars that we plied and the bats that we wielded in the old time, or the murmured talk on the moss-grown bank, as we sat together, building in the summer air castles mightier than Windsor. Ah, they are strong ties, those boyish memories believe me! I remember, as if it were yesterday, my translation of that lovely passage in Persius, beginning— let me see—ah!

"'Quum primum pavido custos mihi purpura cernet,'—

that passage on friendship which gushes out so livingly from the stern heart of the satirist. And when old—complimented me on my verses, my eye sought yours. Verily, I now say as then,—

"'Nescio quod, certe est quod me tibi temperet astrum.'"

["What was the star I know not, but certainly some star it was that attuned me unto thee."]

Audley turned away his head as he returned the grasp of his friend's hand; and while Harley, with his light elastic footstep, descended the stairs, Egerton lingered behind, and there was no trace of the worldly man upon his countenance when he took his place in the carriage by his companion's side.

Two hours afterwards, weary cries of "Question, question!" "Divide, divide!" sank into reluctant silence as Audley Egerton rose to conclude the debate,—the man of men to speak late at night, and to impatient benches: a man who would be heard; whom a Bedlam broke loose would not have roared down; with a voice clear and sound as a bell, and a form as firmly set on the ground as a church-tower. And while, on the dullest of dull questions, Audley Egerton thus, not too lively himself, enforced attention, where was Harley L'Estrange? Standing alone by the river at Richmond, and murmuring low fantastic thoughts as he gazed on the moonlit tide.

When Audley left him at home he had joined his parents, made them gay with his careless gayety, seen the old-fashioned folks retire to rest, and then—while they, perhaps, deemed him once more the hero of ball- rooms and the cynosure of clubs—he drove slowly through the soft summer night, amidst the perfumes of many a garden and many a gleaming chestnut grove, with no other aim before him than to reach the loveliest margin of England's loveliest river, at the hour when the moon was fullest and the song of the nightingale most sweet. And so eccentric a humourist was this man, that I believe, as he there loitered,—no one near to cry "How affected!" or "How romantic!"—he enjoyed himself more than if he had been exchanging the politest "how-d'ye-dos" in the hottest of London drawing-rooms, or betting his hundreds on the odd trick, with Lord de R— — — for his partner.

CHAPTER VII.

Leonard had been about six weeks with his uncle, and those weeks were well spent. Mr. Richard had taken him to his counting-house, and initiated him into business and the mysteries of double entry; and in return for the young man's readiness and zeal in matters which the acute trader instinctively felt were not exactly to his tastes, Richard engaged the best master the town afforded to read with his nephew in the evening. This gentleman was the head usher of a large school, who had his hours to himself after eight o'clock, and was pleased to vary the dull routine of enforced lessons by instructions to a pupil who took delightedly even to the Latin grammar. Leonard made rapid strides, and learned more in those six weeks than many a cleverish boy does in twice as many months. These hours which Leonard devoted to study Richard usually spent from home,— sometimes at the houses of his grand acquaintances in the Abbey Gardens, sometimes in the Reading-Room appropriated to those aristocrats. If he stayed at home, it was in company with his head clerk, and for the purpose of checking his account-books, or looking over the names of doubtful electors.

Leonard had naturally wished to communicate his altered prospects to his old friends, that they, in turn, might rejoice his mother with such good tidings. But he had not been two days in the house before Richard had strictly forbidden all such correspondence.

"Look you," said he, "at present we are on an experiment,—we must see if we like each other. Suppose we don't, you will only have raised expectations in your mother which must end in bitter disappointment; and suppose we do, it will be time enough to write when something definite is settled."

"But my mother will be so anxious—"

"Make your mind easy on that score. I will write regularly to Mr. Dale, and he can tell her that you are well and thriving. No more words, my man,—when I say a thing, I say it." Then, observing that Leonard looked blank and dissatisfied, Richard added, with a good-humoured smile, "I have my reasons for all this—you shall know them later. And I tell you what: if you do as I bid you, it is my intention to settle something handsome on your mother; but if you don't, devil a penny she'll get from me."

With that Richard turned on his heel, and in a few moments his voice was heard loud in objurgation with some of his people.

About the fourth week of Leonard's residence at Mr. Avenel's, his host began to evince a certain change of manner. He was no longer quite so cordial with Leonard, nor did he take the same interest in his progress. About the same period he was frequently caught by the London butler before the looking-glass. He had always been a smart man in his dress, but he was now more particular. He would spoil three white cravats when he went out of an evening, before he could satisfy himself as to the tie. He also bought a 'Peerage,' and it became his favourite study at odd quarters of an hour. All these symptoms proceeded from a cause, and that cause was—woman.

CHAPTER VIII.

The first people at Screwstown were indisputably the Pompleys. Colonel Pompley was grand, but Mrs. Pompley was grander. The colonel was stately in right of his military rank and his services in India; Mrs. Pompley was majestic in right of her connections. Indeed, Colonel Pompley himself would have been crushed under the weight of the dignities which his lady heaped upon him, if he had not been enabled to prop his position with a "connection" of his own. He would never have held his own, nor been permitted to have an independent opinion on matters aristocratic, but for the well-sounding name of his relations, "the Digbies." Perhaps on the principle that obscurity increases the natural size of objects and is an element of the sublime, the colonel did not too accurately define his relations "the Digbies:" he let it be casually understood that they were the Digbies to be found in Debrett. But if some indiscreet Vulgarian (a favourite word with both the Pompleys) asked point-blank if he meant "my Lord Digby," the colonel, with a lofty air, answered, "The elder branch, sir." No one at Screwstown had ever seen these Digbies: they lay amidst the Far, the Recondite,—even to the wife of Colonel Pompley's bosom. Now and then, when the colonel referred to the lapse of years, and the uncertainty of human affections, he would say, "When young Digby and I were boys together," and then add with a sigh, "but we shall never meet again in this world. His family interests secured him a valuable appointment in a distant part of the British dominions." Mrs. Pompley was always rather cowed by the Digbies. She could not be sceptical as to this connection, for the colonel's mother was certainly a Digby, and the colonel impaled the Digby arms. /En revanche/, as the French say, for these marital connections, Mrs. Pompley had her own favourite affinity, which she specially selected from all others when she most desired to produce effect; nay, even upon ordinary occasions the name rose spontaneously to her lips,—the name of the Honourable Mrs. M'Catchley. Was the fashion of a gown or cap admired, her cousin, Mrs. M'Catchley, had just sent to her the pattern from Paris. Was it a question whether the Ministry would stand, Mrs. M'Catchley was in the secret, but Mrs. Pompley had been requested not to say. Did it freeze, "My cousin, Mrs. M'Catchley, had written word that the icebergs at the Pole were supposed to be coming this way." Did the sun glow with more than usual fervour, Mrs. M'Catchley had informed her "that it was Sir Henry Halford's decided opinion that it was on account of the cholera." The good people knew all that was doing at London, at court, in this world—nay, almost in the other—through the medium of the Honourable Mrs. M'Catchley. Mrs. M'Catchley was, moreover, the most elegant of women, the wittiest creature, the dearest. King George the Fourth had presumed to admire Mrs. M'Catehley; but Mrs. M'Catchley, though no prude, let him see that she was proof against the corruptions of a throne. So long had the ears of Mrs. Pompley's friends been filled with the renown of Mrs. M'Catchley, that at last Mrs. M'Catchley was secretly supposed to be a myth, a creature of the elements, a poetic fiction of Mrs. Pompley's. Richard Avenel, however, though by no means a credulous man, was an implicit believer in Mrs. M'Catchley. He had learned that she was a widow, and honourable by birth, and honourable by marriage, living on her handsome jointure, and refusing offers every day that she so lived. Somehow or other, whenever Richard Avenel thought of a wife, he thought of the Honourable Mrs. M'Catchley. Perhaps that romantic attachment to the fair invisible preserved him heart-whole amongst the temptations of Screwstown. Suddenly, to the astonishment of the Abbey Gardens, Mrs. M'Catchley proved her identity, and arrived at Colonel Pompley's in a handsome travelling-carriage, attended by her maid and footman. She had come to stay some weeks; a tea-party was given in her honour. Mr. Avenel and his nephew were invited. Colonel Pompley, who kept his head clear in the midst of the greatest excitement, had a desire to get from the Corporation a lease of a piece of ground adjoining his garden, and he no sooner saw Richard Avenel enter than he caught him by the button, and drew him into a quiet corner, in order to secure his interest. Leonard, meanwhile, was borne on by the stream, till his progress was arrested by a sofa-table at which sat Mrs. M'Catchley herself, with Mrs. Pompley by her side. For on this great occasion the hostess had abandoned her proper post at the entrance, and, whether to show her respect to Mrs. M'Catchley, or to show Mrs. M'Catchley her well-bred contempt for the people of Screwstown, remained in state by her friend, honouring only the elite of the town with introductions to the illustrious visitor.

Mrs. M'Catchley was a very fine woman,—a woman who justified Mrs. Pompley's pride in her. Her cheek-bones were rather high, it is true. but that proved the purity of her Caledonian descent; for the rest, she had a brilliant complexion, heightened by a /soupcon/ of rouge, good eyes and teeth, a showy figure, and all the ladies of Screwstown pronounced her dress to be perfect. She might have arrived at that age at which one intends to stop for the next ten years, but even a Frenchman would not have called her passee,—that is, for a widow. For a spinster it would have been different.

Looking round her with a glass, which Mrs. Pompley was in the habit of declaring that "Mrs. M'Catchley used like an angel," this lady suddenly perceived Leonard Fairfield; and his quiet, simple, thoughtful air and look so contrasted with the stiff beaux to whom she had been presented, that, experienced in fashion as so fine a personage must be supposed to be, she was nevertheless deceived into whispering to Mrs. Pompley,

"That young man has really an /air distingue/; who is he?" "Oh," said
Mrs. Pompley, in unaffected surprise, "that is the nephew of the rich Vulgarian I was telling you of this morning."

"Ah! and you say that he is Mr. Arundel's heir?" "Avenel—not Arundel—my sweet friend."

"Avenel is not a bad name," said Mrs. M'Catchley. "But is the uncle really so rich?"

"The colonel was trying this very day to guess what he is worth; but he says it is impossible to guess it."

"And the young man is his heir?"

"It is thought so; and reading for College, I hear. They say he is clever."

"Present him, my love; I like clever people," said Mrs. M'Catchley, falling back languidly.

About ten minutes afterwards, Richard Avenel having effected his escape from the colonel, and his gaze being attracted towards the sofa-table by the buzz of the admiring crowd, beheld his nephew in animated conversation with the long cherished idol of his dreams. A fierce pang of jealousy shot through his breast. His nephew had never looked so handsome and so intelligent; in fact, poor Leonard had never before been drawn out by a woman of the world, who had learned how to make the most of what little she knew. And as jealousy operates like a pair of bellows on incipient flames, so, at first sight of the smile which the fair widow bestowed upon Leonard, the heart of Mr. Avenel felt in a blaze.

He approached with a step less assured than usual, and, overhearing Leonard's talk, marvelled much at the boy's audacity. Mrs. M'Catchley had been speaking of Scotland and the Waverley Novels, about which Leonard knew nothing. But he knew Burns, and on Burns he grew artlessly eloquent. Burns the poet and peasant—Leonard might well be eloquent on him. Mrs. M'Catchley was amused and pleased with his freshness and naivete, so unlike anything she had ever heard or seen, and she drew him on and on till Leonard fell to quoting. And Richard heard, with less respect for the sentiment than might be supposed, that

"Rank is but the guinea's stamp,
The man's the gowd for a' that."

"Well!" exclaimed Mr. Avenel. "Pretty piece of politeness to tell that to a lady like the Honourable Mrs. M'Catch ley! You'll excuse him, ma'am."

"Sir!" said Mrs. M'Catchley, startled, and lifting her glass. Leonard, rather confused, rose and offered his chair to Richard, who dropped into it. The lady, without waiting for formal introduction, guessed that she saw the rich uncle. "Such a sweet poet-Burns!" said she, dropping her glass. "And it is so refreshing to find so much youthful enthusiasm," she added, pointing her fan towards Leonard, who was receding fast among the crowd.

"Well, he is youthful, my nephew,—rather green!"

"Don't say green!" said Mrs. M'Catchley. Richard blushed scarlet. He was afraid he had committed himself to some expression low and shocking. The lady resumed, "Say unsophisticated."

"A tarnation long word," thought Richard; but he prudently bowed and held his tongue.

"Young men nowadays," continued Mrs. M'Catchley, resettling herself on the sofa, "affect to be so old. They don't dance, and they don't read, and they don't talk much! and a great many of them wear /toupets/ before they are two-and-twenty!"

Richard mechanically passed his hand through his thick curls. But he was still mute; he was still ruefully chewing the cud of the epithet "green." What occult horrid meaning did the word convey to ears polite? Why should he not say "green"?

"A very fine young man your nephew, sir," resumed Mrs. M' Catchley.

Richard grunted.

"And seems full of talent. Not yet at the University? Will he go to Oxford or Cambridge?"

"I have not made up my mind yet if I shall send him to the University at all."

"A young man of his expectations!" exclaimed Mrs. M'Catchley, artfully.

"Expectations!" repeated Richard, firing up. "Has he been talking to you of his expectations?"

"No, indeed, sir. But the nephew of the rich Mr. Avenel! Ah, one hears a great deal, you know, of rich people; it is the penalty of wealth, Mr. Avenel!"

Richard was very much flattered. His crest rose.

"And they say," continued Mrs. M'Catchley, dropping out her words very slowly, as she adjusted her blonde scarf, "that Mr. Avenel has resolved not to marry."

"The devil they do, ma'am!" bolted out Richard, gruffly; and then, ashamed of his /lapsus linguae/, screwed up his lips firmly, and glared on the company with an eye of indignant fire.

Mrs. M'Catchley observed him over her fan. Richard turned abruptly, and she withdrew her eyes modestly, and raised the fan.

"She's a real beauty," said Richard, between his teeth. The fan fluttered.

Five minutes afterwards, the widow and the bachelor seemed so much at their ease that Mrs. Pompley, who had been forced to leave her friend, in order to receive the dean's lady, could scarcely believe her eyes when she returned to the sofa.

Now, it was from that evening that Mr. Richard Avenel exhibited the change of mood which I have described; and from that evening he abstained from taking Leonard with him to any of the parties in the Abbey Gardens.

CHAPTER IX.

Some days after this memorable /soiree/, Colonel Pompley sat alone in his study (which opened pleasantly on an old-fashioned garden), absorbed in the house bills. For Colonel Pompley did not leave that domestic care to his lady,—perhaps she was too grand for it. Colonel Pompley with his own sonorous voice ordered the joints, and with his own heroic hands dispensed the stores. In justice to the colonel, I must add—at whatever risk of offence to the fair sex—that there was not a house at Screwstown so well managed as the Pompleys'; none which so successfully achieved the difficult art of uniting economy with show. I should despair of conveying to you an idea of the extent to which Colonel Pompley made his income go. It was but seven hundred a year; and many a family contrived to do less upon three thousand. To be sure, the Pompleys had no children to sponge upon them. What they had they spent all on themselves. Neither, if the Pompleys never exceeded their income, did they pretend to live much within it. The two ends of the year met at Christmas,—just met, and no more.

Colonel Pompley sat at his desk. He was in his well-brushed blue coat, buttoned across his breast, his gray trousers fitted tight to his limbs, and fastened under his boots with a link chain. He saved a great deal of money in straps. No one ever saw Colonel Pompley in dressing-gown and slippers. He and his house were alike in order—always fit to be seen

"From morn to noon, from noon to dewy eve."

The colonel was a short compact man, inclined to be stout,—with a very red face, that seemed not only shaved, but rasped. He wore his hair cropped close, except just in front, where it formed what the hairdresser called a feather, but it seemed a feather of iron, so stiff and so strong was it. Firmness and precision were emphatically marked on the colonel's countenance. There was a resolute strain on his features, as if he was always employed in making the two ends meet!

So he sat before his house-book, with his steel-pen in his hand, and making crosses here and notes of interrogation there.

"Mrs. M'Catchley's maid," said the colonel to himself, "must be put upon rations. The tea that she drinks! Good heavens!—tea again!"

There was a modest ring at the outer door. "Too early for a visitor!" thought the colonel. "Perhaps it is the water-rates."

The neat man-servant—never seen beyond the offices, save in /grande tenue/, plushed and powdered-entered and bowed. "A gentleman, sir, wishes to see you."

"A gentleman," repeated the colonel, glancing towards the clock. "Are you sure it is a gentleman?"

The man hesitated. "Why, sir, I ben't exactly sure; but he speaks like a gentleman. He do say he comes from London to see you, sir."

A long and interesting correspondence was then being held between the colonel and one of his wife's trustees touching the investment of Mrs. Pompley's fortune. It might be the trustee,—nay, it must be. The trustee had talked of running down to see him.

"Let him come in," said the colonel, "and when I ring—sandwiches and sherry."

"Beef, sir?"

"Ham."

The colonel put aside his house-book, and wiped his pen. In another minute the door opened and the servant announced—

"MR. DIGBY."

The colonel's face fell, and he staggered back.

The door closed, and Mr. Digby stood in the middle of the room, leaning on the great writing-table for support. The poor soldier looked sicklier and shabbier, and nearer the end of all things in life and fortune, than when Lord L'Estrange had thrust the pocket-book into his hands. But still the servant showed knowledge of the world in calling him gentleman; there was no other word to apply to him.

"Sir," began Colonel Pompley, recovering himself, and with great solemnity, "I did not expect this pleasure."

The poor visitor stared round him dizzily, and sank into a chair, breathing hard. The colonel looked as a man only looks upon a poor relation, and buttoned up first one trouser pocket and then the other.

"I thought you were in Canada," said the colonel, at last. Mr. Digby had now got breath to speak, and he said meekly, "The climate would have killed my child, and it is two years since I returned."

"You ought to have found a very good place in England to make it worth your while to leave Canada."

"She could not have lived through another winter in Canada,—the doctor said so."

"Pooh," quoth the colonel.

Mr. Digby drew a long breath. "I would not come to you, Colonel Pompley, while you could think that I came as a beggar for myself."

The colonel's brow relaxed. "A very honourable sentiment, Mr. Digby."

"No: I have gone through a great deal; but you see, Colonel," added the poor relation, with a faint smile, "the campaign is well-nigh over, and peace is at hand."

The colonel seemed touched.

"Don't talk so, Digby,—I don't like it. You are younger than I am— nothing more disagreeable than these gloomy views of things. You have got enough to live upon, you say,—at least so I understand you. I am very glad to hear it; and, indeed, I could not assist you—so many claims on me. So it is all very well, Digby."

"Oh, Colonel Pompley," cried the soldier, clasping his hands, and with feverish energy, "I am a suppliant, not for myself, but my child! I have but one,—only one, a girl. She has been so good to me! She will cost you little. Take her when I die; promise her a shelter, a home. I ask no more. You are my nearest relative. I have no other to look to. You have no children of your own. She will be a blessing to you, as she has been all upon earth to me!"

If Colonel Pompley's face was red in ordinary hours, no epithet sufficiently rubicund or sanguineous can express its colour at this appeal. "The man's mad," he said, at last, with a tone of astonishment that almost concealed his wrath,—"stark mad! I take his child!—lodge and board a great, positive, hungry child! Why, sir, many and many a time have I said to Mrs. Pompley, "T is a mercy we have no children. We could never live in this style if we had children,—never make both ends meet.' Child—the most expensive, ravenous, ruinous thing in the world— a child."

"She has been accustomed to starve," said Mr. Digby, plaintively. "Oh,
Colonel, let me see your wife. Her heart I can touch,—she is a woman."

Unlucky father! A more untoward, unseasonable request the Fates could not have put into his lips.

Mrs. Pompley see the Digbies! Mrs. Pompley learn the condition of the colonel's grand connections! The colonel would never have been his own man again. At the bare idea, he felt as if he could have sunk into the earth with shame. In his alarm he made a stride to the door, with the intention of locking it. Good heavens, if Mrs. Pompley should come in! And the man, too, had been announced by name. Mrs. Pompley might have learned already that a Digby was with her husband,—she might be actually dressing to receive him worthily; there was not a moment to lose.

The colonel exploded. "Sir, I wonder at your impudence. See Mrs. Pompley! Hush, sir, hush!—hold your tongue. I have disowned your connection. I will not have my wife—a woman, sir, of the first family —disgraced by it. Yes; you need not fire up. John Pompley is not a man to be bullied in his own house. I say disgraced. Did not you run into debt, and spend your fortune? Did not you marry a low creature,—a vulgarian, a tradesman's daughter?—-and your poor father such a respectable man,—a benefited clergyman! Did not you sell your commission? Heaven knows what became of the money! Did not you turn (I shudder to say it) a common stage-player, sir? And then, when you were on your last legs, did I not give you L200 out of my own purse to go to Canada? And now here you are again,—and ask me, with a coolness that—that takes away my breath—takes away-my breath, sir—to provide for the child you have thought proper to have,—a child whose connections on the mother's side are of the most abject and discreditable condition. Leave my house, leave it! good heavens, sir, not that way!—this." And the colonel opened the glass-door that led into the garden. "I will let you out this way. If Mrs. Pompley should see you!" And with that thought the colonel absolutely hooked his arm into his poor relation's, and hurried him into the garden.

Mr. Digby said not a word, but he struggled ineffectually to escape from the colonel's arm; and his colour went and came, came and went, with a quickness that showed that in those shrunken veins there were still some drops of a soldier's blood.

But the colonel had now reached a little postern-door in the garden-wall. He opened the latch, and thrust out his poor cousin. Then looking down the lane, which was long, straight, and narrow, and seeing it was quite solitary, his eye fell upon the forlorn man, and remorse shot through his heart. For a moment the hardest of all kinds of avarice, that of the genteel, relaxed its gripe. For a moment the most intolerant of all forms of pride, that which is based upon false pretences, hushed its voice, and the colonel hastily drew out his purse. "There," said he, "that is all I can do for you. Do leave the town as quick as you can, and don't mention your name to any one. Your father was such a respectable man,—beneficed clergyman!"

"And paid for your commission, Mr. Pompley. My name! I am not ashamed of it. But do not fear I shall claim your relationship. No; I am ashamed of you!"

The poor cousin put aside the purse, still stretched towards him, with a scornful hand, and walked firmly down the lane. Colonel Pompley stood irresolute. At that moment a window in his house was thrown open. He heard the noise, turned round, and saw his wife looking out.

Colonel Pompley sneaked back through the shrubbery, hiding himself amongst the trees.

CHAPTER X.

"Ill-luck is a /betise/," said the great Cardinal Richelieu; and in the long run, I fear, his Eminence was right. If you could drop Dick Avenel and Mr. Digby in the middle of Oxford Street,—Dick in a fustian jacket, Digby in a suit of superfine; Dick with five shillings in his pocket, Digby with L1000,—and if, at the end of ten years, you looked up your two men, Dick would be on his road to a fortune, Digby—what we have seen him! Yet Digby had no vice; he did not drink nor gamble. What was he, then? Helpless. He had been an only son,—a spoiled child, brought up as "a gentleman;" that is, as a man who was not expected to be able to turn his hand to anything. He entered, as we have seen, a very expensive regiment, wherein he found himself, at his father's death, with L4000 and the incapacity to say "No." Not naturally extravagant, but without an idea of the value of money,—the easiest, gentlest, best-tempered man whom example ever led astray. This part of his career comprised a very common history,—the poor man living on equal terms with the rich. Debt; recourse to usurers; bills signed sometimes for others, renewed at twenty per cent; the L4000 melted like snow; pathetic appeal to relations; relations have children of their own; small help given grudgingly, eked out by much advice, and coupled with conditions. Amongst the conditions there was a very proper and prudent one,—exchange into a less expensive regiment. Exchange effected; peace; obscure country quarters; ennui, flute-playing, and idleness. Mr. Digby had no resources on a rainy day — except flute-playing; pretty girl of inferior rank; all the officers after her; Digby smitten; pretty girl very virtuous; Digby forms honourable intentions; excellent sentiments; imprudent marriage. Digby falls in life; colonel's lady will not associate with Mrs. Digby; Digby cut by his whole kith and kin; many disagreeable circumstances in regimental life; Digby sells out; love in a cottage; execution in ditto. Digby had been much applauded as an amateur actor; thinks of the stage; genteel comedy,—a gentlemanlike profession. Tries in a provincial town, under another name; unhappily succeeds; life of an actor; hand-to-mouth life; illness; chest affected; Digby's voice becomes hoarse and feeble; not aware of it; attributes failing success to ignorant provincial public; appears in London; is hissed; returns to the provinces; sinks into very small parts; prison; despair; wife dies; appeal again to relations; a subscription made to get rid of him; send him out of the country; place in Canada,—superintendent to an estate, L150 a year; pursued by ill-luck; never before fit for business, not fit now; honest as the day, but keeps slovenly accounts; child cannot bear the winter of Canada; Digby wrapped up in the child; return home; mysterious life for two years; child patient, thoughtful, loving; has learned to work; manages for father; often supports him; constitution rapidly breaking; thought of what will become of his child,—worst disease of all. Poor Digby! never did a base, cruel, unkind thing in his life; and here he is, walking down the lane from Colonel Pompley's house! Now, if Digby had but learned a little of the world's cunning, I think he would have succeeded even with Colonel Pompley. Had he spent the L100 received from Lord L'Estrange with a view to effect; had he bestowed a fitting wardrobe on himself and his pretty Helen; had he stopped at the last stage, taken thence a smart chaise and pair, and presented himself at Colonel Pompley's in a way that would not have discredited the colonel's connection, and then, instead of praying for home and shelter, asked the colonel to become guardian to his child in case of his death, I have a strong notion that the colonel, in spite of his avarice, would have stretched both ends so as to take in Helen Digby. But our poor friend had no such arts. Indeed, of the L100 he had already very little left, for before leaving town he had committed what Sheridan considered the extreme of extravagance,—frittered away his money in paying his debts; and as for dressing up Helen and himself—if that thought had ever occurred to him, he would have rejected it as foolish. He would have thought that the more he showed his poverty, the more he would be pitied,—the worst mistake a poor cousin can commit. According to Theophrastus, the partridge of Paphlagonia has two hearts: so have most men; it is the common mistake of the unlucky to knock at the wrong one.

CHAPTER XI.

Mr. Digby entered the room of the inn in which he had left Helen. She was seated by the window, and looking out wistfully on the narrow street, perhaps at the children at play. There had never been a playtime for Helen Digby.

She sprang forward as her father came in. His coming was her holiday.

"We must go back to London," said Mr. Digby, sinking helplessly on the chair. Then with his sort of sickly smile,—for he was bland even to his child,—"Will you kindly inquire when the first coach leaves?"

All the active cares of their careful life devolved upon that quiet child. She kissed her father, placed before him a cough mixture which he had brought from London, and went out silently to make the necessary inquiries, and prepare for the journey back.

At eight o'clock the father and child were seated in the night-coach, with one other passenger,—a man muffled up to the chin. After the first mile the man let down one of the windows. Though it was summer the air was chill and raw. Digby shivered and coughed.

Helen placed her hand on the window, and, leaning towards the passenger, whispered softly.

"Eh!" said the passenger, "draw up the window? You have got your own window; this is mine. Oxygen, young lady," he added solemnly, "oxygen is the breath of life. Cott, child!" he continued with suppressed choler, and a Welsh pronunciation, "Cott! let us breathe and live."

Helen was frightened, and recoiled.

Her father, who had not heard, or had not heeded, this colloquy, retreated into the corner, put up the collar of his coat, and coughed again.

"It is cold, my dear," said he, languidly, to Helen.

The passenger caught the word, and replied indignantly, but as if soliloquizing,—

"Cold-ugh! I do believe the English are the stuffiest people! Look at their four-post beds—all the curtains drawn, shutters closed, board before the chimney—not a house with a ventilator! Cold-ugh!"

The window next Mr. Digby did not fit well into its frame. "There is a sad draught," said the invalid.

Helen instantly occupied herself in stopping up the chinks of the window with her handkerchief. Mr. Digby glanced ruefully at the other window. The look, which was very eloquent, aroused yet more the traveller's spleen.

"Pleasant!" said he. "Cott! I suppose you will ask me to go outside next! But people who travel in a coach should know the law of a coach. I don't interfere with your window; you have no business to interfere with mine."

"Sir, I did not speak," said Mr. Digby, meekly.

"But Miss here did."

"Ah, sir!" said Helen, plaintively, "if you knew how Papa suffers!" And her hand again moved towards the obnoxious window.

"No, my dear; the gentleman is in his right," said Mr. Digby; and, bowing with his wonted suavity, he added, "Excuse her, sir. She thinks a great deal too much of me."

The passenger said nothing, and Helen nestled closer to her father, and strove to screen him from the air.

The passenger moved uneasily. "Well," said he, with a sort of snort, "air is air, and right is right: but here goes—" and he hastily drew up the window.

Helen turned her face full towards the passenger with a grateful expression, visible even in the dim light.

"You are very kind, sir," said poor Mr. Digby; "I am ashamed to—" his cough choked the rest of the sentence. The passenger, who was a plethoric, sanguineous man, felt as if he were stifling. But he took off his wrappers, and resigned the oxygen like a hero.

Presently he drew nearer to the sufferer, and laid hand on his wrist.

"You are feverish, I fear. I am a medical man. St!—one—two. Cott! you should not travel; you are not fit for it!"

Mr. Digby shook his head; he was too feeble to reply.

The passenger thrust his hand into his coat-pocket, and drew out what seemed a cigar-case, but what, in fact, was a leathern repertory, containing a variety of minute phials.

From one of these phials he extracted two tiny globules. "There," said he, "open your mouth, put those on the tip of your tongue. They will lower the pulse, check the fever. Be better presently, but should not travel, want rest; you should be in bed. Aconite! Henbane! hum! Your papa is of fair complexion,—a timid character, I should say;—a horror of work, perhaps. Eh, child?"

"Sir!" faltered Helen, astonished and alarmed. Was the man a conjuror?

"A case for phosphor!" cried the passenger: "that fool Browne would have said arsenic. Don't be persuaded to take arsenic!"

"Arsenic, sir!" echoed the mild Digby. "No: however unfortunate a man may be, I think, sir, that suicide is—tempting, perhaps, but highly criminal."

"Suicide," said the passenger, tranquilly,—"suicide is my hobby! You have no symptom of that kind, you say?"

"Good heavens! No, sir."

"If ever you feel violently impelled to drown yourself, take pulsatilla; but if you feel a preference towards blowing out your brains, accompanied with weight in the limbs, loss of appetite, dry cough, and bad corns, /sulphuret of antimony/. Don't forget."

Though poor Mr. Digby confusedly thought that the gentleman was out of his mind, yet he tried politely to say "that he was much obliged, and would be sure to remember; "but his tongue failed him, and his own ideas grew perplexed. His head fell back heavily, and he sank into a silence which seemed that of sleep.

The traveller looked hard at Helen, as she gently drew her father's head on her shoulder, and there pillowed it with a tenderness which was more that of a mother than child.

"Moral affections, soft, compassionate!—a good child and would go well with—/pulsatilla/."

Helen held up her finger, and glanced from her father to the traveller, and then to her father again.

"Certainly,—pulsatilla!" muttered the homoeopathist, and ensconcing himself in his own corner, he also sought to sleep. But after vain efforts, accompanied by restless gestures and movements, he suddenly started up, and again extracted his phial-book.

"What the deuce are they to me?" he muttered. "Morbid sensibility of character—coffee? No!—accompanied by vivacity and violence—nux!" He brought his book to the window, contrived to read the label on a pigmy bottle. "Nux! that's it," he said,—and he swallowed a globule!

"Now," quoth he, after a pause, "I don't care a straw for the misfortunes of other people; nay, I have half a mind to let down the window."

Helen looked up.

"But I'll not," he added resolutely; and this time he fell fairly asleep.

CHAPTER XII.

The coach stopped at eleven o'clock to allow the passengers to sup. The homoeopathist woke up, got out, gave himself a shake, and inhaled the fresh air into his vigorous lungs with an evident sensation of delight. He then turned and looked into the coach.

"Let your father get out, my dear," said he, with a tone more gentle than usual. "I should like to see him indoors,—perhaps I can do him good."

But what was Helen's terror when she found that her father did not stir! He was in a deep swoon, and still quite insensible when they lifted him from the carriage. When he recovered his senses his cough returned, and the effort brought up blood.

It was impossible for him to proceed farther. The homoeopathist assisted to undress and put him into bed. And having administered another of his mysterious globules, he inquired of the landlady how far it was to the nearest doctor,—for the inn stood by itself in a small hamlet. There was the parish apothecary three miles off. But on hearing that the gentlefolks employed Dr. Dosewell, and it was a good seven miles to his house, the homoeopathist fetched a deep breath. The coach only stopped a quarter of an hour.

"Cott!" said he, angrily, to himself, "the nux was a failure. My sensibility is chronic. I must go through a long course to get rid of it. Hollo, guard! get out my carpet-bag. I sha'n't go on to-night."

And the good man after a very slight supper went upstairs again to the sufferer.

"Shall I send for Dr. Dosewell, sir?" asked the landlady, stopping him at the door.

"Hum! At what hour to-morrow does the next coach to London pass?"

"Not before eight, sir."

"Well, send for the doctor to be here at seven. That leaves us at least some hours free from allopathy and murder," grunted the disciple of Hahnemann, as he entered the room.

Whether it was the globule that the homoeopathist had administered, or the effect of nature, aided by repose, that checked the effusion of blood, and restored some temporary strength to the poor sufferer, is more than it becomes one not of the Faculty to opine. But certainly Mr. Digby seemed better, and he gradually fell into a profound sleep, but not till the doctor had put his ear to his chest, tapped it with his hand, and asked several questions; after which the homoeopathist retired into a corner of the room, and leaning his face on his hand seemed to meditate. From his thoughts he was disturbed by a gentle touch. Helen was kneeling at his feet. "Is he very ill, very?" said she; and her fond wistful eyes were fixed on the physician's with all the earnestness of despair.

"Your father is very ill," replied the doctor, after a short pause. "He cannot move hence for some days at least. I am going to London; shall I call on your relations, and tell some of them to join you?"

"No, thank you, sir," answered Helen, colouring. "But do not fear; I can nurse Papa. I think he has been worse before,—that is, he has complained more."

The homeeopathist rose, and took two strides across the room; then he paused by the bed, and listened to the breathing of the sleeping man.

He stole back to the child, who was still kneeling, took her in his arms and kissed her. "Tamn it," said he, angrily, and putting her down, "go to bed now,—you are not wanted any more."

"Please, sir," said Helen, "I cannot leave him so. If he wakes he would miss me."

The doctor's hand trembled; he had recourse to his globules.

"Anxiety—grief suppressed," muttered he. "Don't you want to cry, my dear? Cry,—do!"

"I can't," murmured Helen.

"Pulsatilla!" said the doctor, almost with triumph. "I said so from the first. Open your mouth—here! Goodnight. My room is opposite,—No. 6; call me if he wakes."

CHAPTER XIII.

At seven o'clock Dr. Dosewell arrived, and was shown into the room of the homoeopathist, who, already up and dressed, had visited his patient.

"My name is Morgan," said the homoeopathist; "I am a physician. I leave in your hands a patient whom, I fear, neither I nor you can restore. Come and look at him."

The two doctors went into the sick-room. Mr. Digby was very feeble, but he had recovered his consciousness, and inclined his head courteously.

"I am sorry to cause so much trouble," said he. The homoeopathist drew away Helen; the allopathist seated himself by the bedside and put his questions, felt the pulse, sounded the lungs, and looked at the tongue of the patient. Helen's eye was fixed on the strange doctor, and her colour rose, and her eye sparkled when he got up cheerfully, and said in a pleasant voice, "You may have a little tea."

"Tea!" growled the homceopathist,—"barbarian!"

"He is better, then, sir?" said Helen, creeping to the allopathist.

"Oh, yes, my dear,—certainly; and we shall do very well, I hope."

The two doctors then withdrew.

"Last about a week!" said Dr. Dosewell, smiling pleasantly, and showing a very white set of teeth.

"I should have said a month; but our systems are different," replied Dr.
Morgan, dryly.

DR. DOSEWELL (courteously).—"We country doctors bow to our metropolitan superiors; what would you advise? You would venture, perhaps, the experiment of bleeding."

DR. MORGAN (spluttering and growling Welsh, which he never did but in excitement).—"Pleed! Cott in heaven! do you think I am a putcher,—an executioner? Pleed! Never."

DR. DOSEWELL.—"I don't find it answer, myself, when both lungs are gone!
But perhaps you are for inhaling?"

DR. MORGAN.—"Fiddledee!"

DR. DOSEWELL (with some displeasure).—"What would you advise, then, in order to prolong our patient's life for a month?"

DR. MORGAN.—"Give him Rhus!"

DR. DOSEWELL.—"Rhus, sir! Rhus! I don't know that medicine. Rhus!"

Dr. MORGAN.—"Rhus Toxicodendron."

The length of the last word excited Dr. Dosewell's respect. A word of five syllables,—that was something like! He bowed deferentially, but still looked puzzled. At last he said, smiling frankly, "You great London practitioners have so many new medicines: may I ask what Rhus toxico—toxico— "

"Dendron."

"Is?"

"The juice of the upas,—vulgarly called the poison-tree." Dr. Dosewell started.

"Upas—poison-tree—little birds that come under the shade fall down dead! You give upas juice in these desperate cases: what's the dose?"

Dr. Morgan grinned maliciously, and produced a globule the size of a small pin's head.

Dr. Dosewell recoiled in disgust.

"Oh!" said he, very coldly, and assuming at once an air of superb superiority, "I see, a homoeopathist, sir!"

"A homoeopathist."

"Um!"

"Um!"

"A strange system, Dr. Morgan," said Dr. Dosewell, recovering his cheerful smile, but with a curl of contempt in it, "and would soon do for the druggists."

"Serve 'em right. The druggists soon do for the patients."

"Sir!"

"Sir!"

DR. DOSEWELL (with dignity).—-"You don't know, perhaps, Dr. Morgan, that I am an apothecary as well as a surgeon. In fact," he added, with a certain grand humility, "I have not yet taken a diploma, and am but doctor by courtesy."

DR. MORGAN.—"All one, sir! Doctor signs the death-warrant, 'pothecary does the deed!"

DR. DOSEWELL (with a withering sneer).—"Certainly we don't profess to keep a dying man alive upon the juice of the deadly upas-tree."

DR. MORGAN (complacently).—"Of course you don't. There are no poisons with us. That's just the difference between you and me, Dr. Dosewell."

DR. DOSEWELL (pointing to the homceopathist's travelling pharmacopoeia, and with affected candour).—"Indeed, I have always said that if you can do no good, you can do no harm, with your infinitesimals."

DR. MORGAN, who had been obtuse to the insinuation of poisoning, fires up violently at the charge of doing no harm. "You know nothing about it! I could kill quite as many people as you, if I chose it; but I don't choose."

DR. DOSEWELL (shrugging his shoulders).—"Sir Sir! It is no use arguing; the thing's against common-sense. In short, it is my firm belief that it is—is a complete—"

DR. MORGAN.—"A complete what?"

DR. DOSEWELL (provoked to the utmost).—"Humbug!"

DR. MORGAN.—"Humbug! Cott in heaven! You old—"

DR. DOSEWELL.—"Old what, sir?"

DR. MORGAN (at home in a series of alliteral vowels, which none but a Cymbrian could have uttered without gasping).—"Old allopathical anthropophagite!"

DR. DOSEWELL (starting up, seizing by the back the chair on which he had sat, and bringing it down violently on its four legs).—"Sir!"

DR. MORGAN (imitating the action with his own chair).—"Sir!"

DR. DOSEWELL.—"You're abusive."

DR. MORGAN.—"You're impertinent."

DR. DOSEWELL.—" Sir!"

DR. MORGAN.—"Sir!"

The two rivals confronted each other.

They were both athletic men, and fiery men. Dr. Dosewell was the taller, but Dr. Morgan was the stouter. Dr. Dosewell on the mother's side was Irish; but Dr. Morgan on both sides was Welsh. All things considered, I would have backed Dr. Morgan if it had come to blows. But, luckily for the honour of science, here the chambermaid knocked at the door, and said, "The coach is coming, sir."

Dr. Morgan recovered his temper and his manners at that announcement.

"Dr. Dosewell," said he, "I have been too hot,—I apologize."

"Dr. Morgan," answered the allopathist, "I forgot myself. Your hand, sir."

DR. MORGAN.—"We are both devoted to humanity, though with different opinions. We should respect each other."

DR. DOSEWELL.—"Where look for liberality, if men of science are illiberal to their brethren?"

DR. MORGAN (aside).—"The old hypocrite! He would pound me in a mortar if the law would let him."

DR. DOSEWELL (aside).—"The wretched charlatan! I should like to pound him in a mortar."

DR. MORGAN.—"Good-by, my esteemed and worthy brother."

DR. DOSEWELL.—"My excellent friend, good-by."

DR. MORGAN (returning in haste).—"I forgot. I don't think our poor patient is very rich. I confide him to your disinterested benevolence." (Hurries away.)

DR. DOSEWELL (in a rage).—"Seven miles at six o'clock in the morning, and perhaps done out of my fee! Quack! Villain!"

Meanwhile, Dr. Morgan had returned to the sick-room.

"I must wish you farewell," said he to poor Mr. Digby, who was languidly sipping his tea. "But you are in the hands of a—of a—gentleman in the profession."

"You have been too kind,—I am shocked," said Mr. Digby. "Helen, where's my purse?"

Dr. Morgan paused.

He paused, first, because it must be owned that his practice was restricted, and a fee gratified the vanity natural to unappreciated talent, and had the charm of novelty, which is sweet to human nature itself. Secondly, he was a man—

"Who knew his rights; and, knowing, dared maintain."

He had resigned a coach fare, stayed a night, and thought he had relieved his patient. He had a right to his fee.

On the other hand, he paused, because, though he had small practice, he was tolerably well off, and did not care for money in itself, and he suspected his patient to be no Croesus.

Meanwhile the purse was in Helen's hand. He took it from her, and saw but a few sovereigns within the well-worn network. He drew the child a little aside.

"Answer me, my dear, frankly,—is your papa rich?—" And he glanced at the shabby clothes strewed on the chair and Helen's faded frock.

"Alas, no!" said Helen, hanging her head. "Is that all you have?"

"All."

"I am ashamed to offer you two guineas," said Mr. Digby's hollow voice from the bed.

"And I should be still more ashamed to take them. Good by, sir. Come here, my child. Keep your money, and don't waste it on the other doctor more than you can help. His medicines can do your father no good. But I suppose you must have some. He's no physician, therefore there's no fee. He'll send a bill,—it can't be much. You understand. And now, God bless you."

Dr. Morgan was off. But, as he paid the landlady his bill, he said considerately, "The poor people upstairs can pay you, but not that doctor,—and he's of no use. Be kind to the little girl, and get the doctor to tell his patient (quietly of course) to write to his friends—soon—you understand. Somebody must take charge of the poor child. And stop—hold your hand; take care—these globules for the little girl when her father dies,"—here the doctor muttered to himself, "grief,—aconite, and if she cries too much afterwards, these—(don't mistake). Tears,— caustic!"

"Come, sir," cried the coachman.

"Coming; tears,—caustic," repeated the homoeopathist, pulling out his handkerchief and his phial-book together as he got into the coach; and he hastily swallowed his antilachrymal.

CHAPTER XIV.

Richard Avenel was in a state of great nervous excitement. He proposed to give an entertainment of a kind wholly new to the experience of Screwstown. Mrs. M'Catchley had described with much eloquence the /Dejeunes dansants/ of her fashionable friends residing in the elegant suburbs of Wimbledon and Fulham. She declared that nothing was so agreeable. She had even said point-blank to Mr. Avenel, "Why don't you give a /Dejeune dansant/?" And, therewith, a /Dejeune dansant/ Mr. Avenel resolved to give.

The day was fixed, and Mr. Avenel entered into all the requisite preparations, with the energy of a man and the providence of a woman.

One morning as he stood musing on the lawn, irresolute as to the best site for the tents, Leonard came up to him with an open letter in his hand.

"My dear uncle," said he, softly.

"Ha!" exclaimed Mr. Avenel, with a start. "Ha-well, what now?"

"I have just received a letter from Mr. Dale. He tells me that my poor mother is very restless and uneasy, because he cannot assure her that he has heard from me; and his letter requires an answer. Indeed I shall seem very ungrateful to him—to all—if I do not write."

Richard Avenel's brows met. He uttered an impatient "Pish!" and turned away. Then coming back, he fixed his clear hawk-like eye on Leonard's ingenuous countenance, linked his arm into his nephew's, and drew him into the shrubbery.

"Well, Leonard," said he, after a pause, "it is time that I should give you some idea of my plans with regard to you. You have seen my manner of living—some difference from what you ever saw before, I calculate! Now I have given you, what no one gave me, a lift in the world; and where I place you, there you must help yourself."

"Such is my duty and my desire," said Leonard, heartily. "Good. You are a clever lad, and a genteel lad, and will do me credit. I have had doubts of what is best for you. At one time I thought of sending you to college. That, I know; is Mr. Dale's wish; perhaps it is your own. But I have given up that idea; I have something better for you. You have a clear head for business, and are a capital arithmetician. I think of bringing you up to superintend my business; by and by I will adinit you into partnership; and before you are thirty you will be a rich man. Come, does that suit you?"

"My dear uncle," said Leonard, frankly, but much touched by this generosity, "it is not for me to have a choice. I should have preferred going to college, because there I might gain independence for myself and cease to be a burden on you. Moreover, my heart moves me to studies more congenial with the college than the counting-house. But all this is nothing compared with my wish to be of use to you, and to prove in any way, however feebly, my gratitude for all your kindness."

"You're a good, grateful, sensible lad," exclaimed Richard, heartily; "and believe me, though I'm a rough diamond, I have your true interest at heart. You can be of use to me, and in being so you will best serve yourself. To tell you the truth, I have some idea of changing my condition. There's a lady of fashion and quality who, I think, may condescend to become Mrs. Avenel; and if so, I shall probably reside a great part of the year in London. I don't want to give up my business. No other investment will yield the same interest. But you can soon learn to superintend it for me, as some day or other I may retire, and then you can step in. Once a member of our great commercial class, and with your talents you may be anything,—member of parliament, and after that, minister of State, for what I know. And my wife—hem! that is to be—has great connections, and you shall marry well; and—oh, the Avenels will hold their heads with the highest, after all! Damn the aristocracy! we clever fellows will be the aristocrats, eh?" Richard rubbed his hands.

Certainly, as we have seen, Leonard, especially in his earlier steps to knowledge, had repined at his position in the many degrees of life; certainly he was still ambitious; certainly he could not now have returned contentedly to the humble occupation he had left;

and woe to the young man who does not hear with a quickened pulse and brightening eye words that promise independence, and flatter with the hope of distinction. Still, it was with all the reaction of chill and mournful disappointment that Leonard, a few hours after this dialogue with his uncle, found himself alone in the fields, and pondering over the prospects before him. He had set his heart upon completing his intellectual education, upon developing those powers within him which yearned for an arena of literature, and revolted from the routine of trade.

But to his credit be it said, that he vigorously resisted this natural disappointment, and by degrees schooled himself to look cheerfully on the path imposed on his duty, and sanctioned by the manly sense that was at the core of his character.

I believe that this self-conquest showed that the boy had true genius.
The false genius would have written sonnets and despaired.

But still, Richard Avenel left his nephew sadly perplexed as to the knotty question from which their talk on the future had diverged,—namely, should he write to the parson, and assure the fears of his mother? How do so without Richard's consent, when Richard had on a former occasion so imperiously declared that, if he did, it would lose his mother all that Richard intended to settle on her? While he was debating this matter with his conscience, leaning against a stile that interrupted a path to the town, Leonard Fairfield was startled by an exclamation. He looked up, and beheld Mr. Sprott the tinker.

CHAPTER XV.

The tinker, blacker and grimmer than ever, stared hard at the altered person of his old acquaintance, and extended his sable fingers, as if inclined to convince himself by the sense of touch that it was Leonard in the flesh that he beheld, under vestments so marvellously elegant and preternaturally spruce.

Leonard shrank mechanically from the contact, while in great surprise he faltered,—

"You here, Mr. Sprott! What could bring you so far from home?"

"'Ome!" echoed the tinker, "I 'as no 'ome! or rather, d' ye see, Muster Fairfilt, I makes myself at 'ome verever I goes! Lor' love ye! I ben't settled on no parridge. I wanders here and I vanders there, and that's my 'ome verever I can mend my kettles and sell my tracks!"

So saying, the tinker slid his panniers on the ground, gave a grunt of release and satisfaction, and seated himself with great composure on the stile from which Leonard had retreated.

"But, dash my wig," resumed Mr. Sprott, as he once more surveyed Leonard, "vy, you bees a rale gentleman, now, surely! Vot's the dodge, eh?"

"Dodge!" repeated Leonard, mechanically, "I don't understand you." Then, thinking that it was neither necessary nor expedient to keep up his acquaintance with Mr. Sprott, nor prudent to expose himself to the battery of questions which he foresaw that further parley would bring upon him, he extended a crown-piece to the tinker; and saying, with a half-smile, "You must excuse me for leaving you—I have business in the town; and do me the favour to accept this trifle," he walked briskly off.

The tinker looked long at the crown-piece, and then sliding it into his pocket, said to himself,—

"Ho, 'ush-money! No go, my swell cove."

After venting that brief soliloquy he sat silent a little while, till Leonard was nearly out of sight; then rose, resumed his fardel, and creeping quick along the hedgerows, followed Leonard towards the town. Just in the last field, as he looked over the hedge, he saw Leonard accosted by a gentleman of comely mien and important swagger. That gentleman soon left the young man, and came, whistling loud, up the path, and straight towards the tinker. Mr. Sprott looked round, but the hedge was too neat to allow of a good hiding-place, so he put a bold front on it, and stepped forth like a man. But, alas for him! before he got into the public path, the proprietor of the land, Mr. Richard Avenel (for the gentleman was no less a personage), had spied out the trespasser, and called to him with a "Hillo, fellow," that bespoke all the dignity of a man who owns acres, and all the wrath of a man who beholds those acres impudently invaded.

The tinker stopped, and Mr. Avenel stalked up to him. "What the devil are you doing on my property, lurking by my hedge? I suspect you are an incendiary!"

"I be a tinker," quoth Mr. Sprott, not louting low, for a sturdy republican was Mr. Sprott, but, like a lord of human kind,—

"Pride in his port, defiance in his eye."

Mr. Avenel's fingers itched to knock the tinker's villanous hat off his jacobinical head, but he repressed the undignified impulse by thrusting both hands deep into his trousers' pockets.

"A tinker!" he cried,—"that's a vagrant; and I'm a magistrate, and I've a great mind to send you to the treadmill,—that I have. What do you do here, I say? You have not answered my question."

"What does I do 'ere?" said Mr. Sprott. "Vy, you had better ax my crakter of the young gent I saw you talking with just now; he knows me."

"What! my nephew knows you?"

"W-hew," whistled the tinker, "your nephew is it, sir? I have a great respek for your family. I 've knowed Mrs. Fairfilt the vasher-voman this many a year. I 'umbly ax your pardon." And he took off his hat this time.

Mr. Avenel turned red and white in a breath. He growled out something inaudible, turned on his heel, and strode off. The tinker watched him as he had watched Leonard, and then dogged the uncle as he had dogged the nephew. I don't presume to say that there was cause and effect in what happened that night, but it was what is called "a curious coincidence" that that night one of Richard Avenel's ricks was set on fire, and that that day he had called Mr. Sprott an incendiary. Mr. Sprott was a man of a very high spirit, and did not forgive an insult easily. His nature was inflammatory, and so was that of the lucifers which he always carried about him, with his tracts and glue-pots.

The next morning there was an inquiry made for the tinker, but he had disappeared from the neighbourhood.

CHAPTER XVI.

It was a fortunate thing that the dejeune dansant so absorbed Mr. Richard Avenel's thoughts that even the conflagration of his rick could not scare away the graceful and poetic images connected with that pastoral festivity. He was even loose and careless in the questions he put to Leonard about the tinker; nor did he send justice in pursuit of that itinerant trader; for, to say truth, Richard Avenel was a man accustomed to make enemies amongst the lower orders; and though he suspected Mr. Sprott of destroying his rick, yet, when he once set about suspecting, he found he had quite as good cause to suspect fifty other persons. How on earth could a man puzzle himself about ricks and tinkers when all his cares and energies were devoted to a /dejeune dansant/? It was a maxim of Richard Avenel's, as it ought to be of every clever man, "to do one thing at a time;" and therefore he postponed all other considerations till the /dejeune dansant/ was fairly done with. Amongst these considerations was the letter which Leonard wished to write to the parson. "Wait a bit, and we will both write!" said Richard, good- humouredly, "the moment the dijeune dansant is over!"

It must be owned that this fete was no ordinary provincial ceremonial.
Richard Avenel was a man to do a thing well when he set about it,—

"He soused the cabbage with a bounteous heart."

By little and little his first notions had expanded, till what had been meant to be only neat and elegant now embraced the costly and magnificent. Artificers accustomed to /dejeunes dansants/ came all the way from London to assist, to direct, to create. Hungarian singers and Tyrolese singers and Swiss peasant-women, who were to chant the /Ranz des Vaches/, and milk cows or make syllabubs, were engaged. The great marquee was decorated as a Gothic banquet-hall; the breakfast itself was to consist of "all the delicacies of the season." In short, as Richard Avenel said to himself, "It is a thing once in a way; a thing on which I don't object to spend money, provided that the thing is—the thing!"

It had been a matter of grave meditation how to make the society worthy of the revel; for Richard Avenel was not contented with the mere aristocracy of the town,—his ambition had grown with his expenses. "Since it will cost so much," said he, "I may as well come it strong, and get in the county."

True, that he was personally acquainted with very few of what are called county families. But still, when a man makes himself a mark in a large town, and can return one of the members whom that town sends to parliament; and when, moreover, that man proposes to give some superb and original entertainment, in which the old can eat and the young can dance, there is no county in the island that has not families enow who will be delighted by an invitation from THAT MAN. And so Richard, finding that, as the thing got talked of, the dean's lady, and Mrs. Pompley, and various other great personages, took the liberty to suggest that Squire this, and Sir somebody that, would be so pleased if they were asked, fairly took the bull by the horns, and sent out his cards to Park, Hall, and Rectory, within a circumference of twelve miles. He met with but few refusals, and he now counted upon five hundred guests.

"In for a penny in for a pound," said Mr. Richard Avenel. "I wonder what Mrs. M'Catchley will say?" Indeed, if the whole truth must be known,— Mr. Richard Avenel not only gave that /dejeune dansant/ in honour of Mrs. M'Catchley, but he had fixed in his heart of hearts upon that occasion (when surrounded by all his splendour, and assisted by the seductive arts of Terpsichore and Bacchus) to whisper to Mrs. M'Catchley those soft words which—but why not here let Mr. Richard Avenel use his own idiomatic and unsophisticated expression? "Please the pigs, then," said Mr. Avenel to himself, "I shall pop the question!"

CHAPTER XVII.

The Great Day arrived at last; and Mr. Richard Avenel, from his dressing- room window, looked on the scene below as Hannibal or Napoleon looked from the Alps on Italy. It was a scene to gratify the thought of conquest, and reward the labours of ambition. Placed on a little eminence stood the singers from the mountains of the Tyrol, their high- crowned hats and filigree buttons and gay sashes gleaming in the sun. Just seen from his place of watch, though concealed from the casual eye, the Hungarian musicians lay in ambush amidst a little belt of laurels and American shrubs. Far to the right lay what had once been called /horresco referens/ the duckpond, where—"Dulce sonant tenui gutture carmen aves." But the ruthless ingenuity of the head-artificer had converted the duck-pond into a Swiss lake, despite grievous wrong and sorrow to the /assuetum innocuumque genus/,—the familiar and harmless inhabitants, who had been all expatriated and banished from their native waves. Large poles twisted with fir branches, stuck thickly around the lake, gave to the waters the becoming Helvetian gloom. And here, beside three cows all bedecked with ribbons, stood the Swiss maidens destined to startle the shades with the /Ranz des Vaches/. To the left, full upon the sward, which it almost entirely covered, stretched the great Gothic marquee, divided into two grand sections,—one for the dancing, one for the dejeune.

The day was propitious,—not a cloud in the sky. The musicians were already tuning their instruments; figures of waiters hired of Gunter— trim and decorous, in black trousers and white waistcoats—passed to and fro the space between the house and marquee. Richard looked and looked; and as he looked he drew mechanically his razor across the strop; and when he had looked his fill, he turned reluctantly to the glass and shaved! All that blessed morning he had been too busy, till then, to think of shaving.

There is a vast deal of character in the way that a man performs that operation of shaving! You should have seen Richard Avenel shave! You could have judged at once how he would shave his neighbours, when you saw the celerity, the completeness with which he shaved himself,—a forestroke and a backstroke, and /tondenti barba cadebat/. Cheek and chin were as smooth as glass. You would have buttoned up your pockets instinctively if you had seen him.

But the rest of Mr. Avenel's toilet was not completed with correspondent despatch. On his bed, and on his chairs, and on his sofa, and on his drawers, lay trousers and vests and cravats enough to distract the choice of a Stoic. And first one pair of trousers was tried on, and then another—and one waistcoat, and then a second, and then a third. Gradually that chef-d'oeuvre of civilization—a man dressed—grew into development and form; and, finally, Mr. Richard Avenel emerged into the light of day. He had been lucky in his costume,—he felt it. It might not suit every one in colour or cut, but it suited him.

And this was his garb. On such occasion, what epic poet would not describe the robe and tunic of a hero?

His surtout—in modern phrase his frockcoat—was blue, a rich blue, a blue that the royal brothers of George the Fourth were wont to favour. And the surtout, single-breasted, was thrown open gallantly; and in the second button-hole thereof was a moss-rose. The vest was white, and the trousers a pearl gray, with what tailors style "a handsome fall over the boot." A blue and white silk cravat, tied loose and debonair; an ample field of shirt front, with plain gold studs; a pair of lemon-coloured kid gloves, and a white hat, placed somewhat too knowingly on one side, complete the description, and "give the world assurance of the man." And, with his light, firm, well-shaped figure, his clear complexion, his keen, bright eye, and features that bespoke the courage, precision, and alertness of his character,—that is to say, features bold, not large, well-defined, and regular,—you might walk long through town or country before you would see a handsomer specimen of humanity than our friend Richard Avenel.

Handsome, and feeling that he was handsome; rich, and feeling that he was rich; lord of the fete, and feeling that he was lord of the fete, Richard Avenel stepped out upon his lawn.

And now the dust began to rise along the road, and carriages and gigs and chaises and flies might be seen at near intervals and in quick procession. People came pretty much about the same time-as they do in the country—Heaven reward them for it!

Richard Avenel was not quite at his ease at first in receiving his guests, especially those whom he did not know by sight. But when the dancing began, and he had secured the fair hand of Mrs. M'Catchley for the initiary quadrille, his courage and presence of mind returned to him; and, seeing that many people whom he had not received at all seemed to enjoy themselves very much, he gave up the attempt to receive those who came after,—and that was a great relief to all parties.

Meanwhile Leonard looked on the animated scene with a silent melancholy, which he in vain endeavoured to shake off,—a melancholy more common amongst very young men in such scenes than we are apt to suppose. Somehow or other, the pleasure was not congenial to him; he had no Mrs. M'Catchley to endear it; he knew very few people, he was shy, he felt his position with his uncle was equivocal, he had not the habit of society, he heard, incidentally, many an ill-natured remark upon his uncle and the entertainment, he felt indignant and mortified. He had been a great deal happier eating his radishes and reading his book by the little fountain in Riccabocca's garden. He retired to a quiet part of the grounds, seated himself under a tree, leaned his cheek on his hand, and mused. He was soon far away;—happy age, when, whatever the present, the future seems so fair and so infinite!

But now the dejeune had succeeded the earlier dances; and, as champagne flowed royally, it is astonishing how the entertainment brightened.

The sun was beginning to slope towards the west, when, during a temporary cessation of the dance, all the guests had assembled in such space as the tent left on the lawn, or thickly filled the walks immediately adjoining it. The gay dresses of the ladies, the joyous laughter heard everywhere, and the brilliant sunlight over all, conveyed even to Leonard the notion, not of mere hypocritical pleasure, but actual healthful happiness. He was attracted from his revery, and timidly mingled with the groups. But Richard Avenel, with the fair Mrs. M'Catchley—her complexion more vivid, and her eyes more dazzling, and her step more elastic than usual—had turned from the gayety just as Leonard had turned towards it, and was now on the very spot (remote, obscure, shaded by the few trees above five years old that Mr. Avenel's property boasted) which the young dreamer had deserted.

And then! Ah, then! moment so meet for the sweet question of questions, place so appropriate for the delicate, bashful, murmured popping thereof!—-suddenly from the sward before, from the groups beyond, there floated to the ears of Richard Avenel an indescribable, mingled, ominous sound,—a sound as of a general titter, a horrid, malignant, but low cachinnation. And Mrs. M'Catchley, stretching forth her parasol, exclaimed, "Dear me, Mr. Avenel, what can they be all crowding there for?"

There are certain sounds and certain sights—the one indistinct, the other vaguely conjecturable—which, nevertheless, we know, by an instinct, bode some diabolical agency at work in our affairs. And if any man gives an entertainment, and hears afar a general, ill-suppressed, derisive titter, and sees all his guests hurrying towards one spot, I defy him to remain unmoved and uninquisitive. I defy him still more to take that precise occasion (however much he may have before designed it) to drop gracefully on his right knee before the handsomest Mrs. M'Catchley in the universe, and—pop the question! Richard Avenel blurted out something very like an oath; and, half guessing that something must have happened that it would not be pleasing to bring immediately under the notice of Mrs. M'Catchley, he said hastily, "Excuse me. I'll just go and see what is the matter; pray, stay till I come back." With that he sprang forward; in a minute he was in the midst of the group, that parted aside with the most obliging complacency to make way for him.

"But what's the matter?" he asked impatiently, yet fearfully. Not a voice answered. He strode on, and beheld his nephew in the arms of a woman!

"God bless my soul!" said Richard Avenel.

CHAPTER XVIII.

And such a woman!

She had on a cotton gown,—very neat, I dare say, for an under-housemaid; and such thick shoes! She had on a little black straw bonnet; and a kerchief, that might have cost tenpence, pinned across her waist instead of a shawl; and she looked altogether-respectable, no doubt, but exceedingly dusty! And she was hanging upon Leonard's neck, and scolding, and caressing, and crying very loud. "God bless my soul!" said Mr. Richard Avenel.

And as he uttered that innocent self-benediction, the woman hastily turned round, and darting from Leonard, threw herself right upon Richard Avenel—burying under her embrace blue-coat, moss rose, white waistcoat and all—with a vehement sob and a loud exclamation!

"Oh! brother Dick!—dear, dear brother Dick! And I lives to see thee agin!" And then came two such kisses—you might have heard them a mile off! The situation of brother Dick was appalling; and the crowd, that had before only tittered politely, could not now resist the effect of this sudden embrace. There was a general explosion! It was a roar! That roar would have killed a weak man; but it sounded to the strong heart of Richard Avenel like the defiance of a foe, and it plucked forth in an instant from all conventional let and barrier the native spirit of the Anglo-Saxon.

He lifted abruptly his handsome masculine head, and looked round the ring of his ill-bred visitors with a haughty stare of rebuke and surprise.

"Ladies and gentlemen," then said he, very coolly, "I don't see what there is to laugh at! A brother and sister meet after many years' separation, and the sister cries, poor thing. For my part I think it very natural that she should cry; but not that you should laugh!"

In an instant the whole shame was removed from Richard Avenel, and rested in full weight upon the bystanders. It is impossible to say how foolish and sheepish they all looked, nor how slinkingly each tried to creep off.

Richard Avenel seized his advantage with the promptitude of a man who had got on in America, and was, therefore, accustomed to make the best of things. He drew Mrs. Fairfield's arm in his, and led her into the house; but when he had got her safe into his parlour—Leonard following all the time—and the door was closed upon those three, then Richard Avenel's ire burst forth.

"You impudent, ungrateful, audacious—drab!"

Yes, drab was the word. I am shocked to say it, but the duties of a historian are stern: and the word was drab.

"Drab!" faltered poor Jane Fairfield; and she clutched hold of Leonard to save herself from falling.

"Sir!" cried Leonard, fiercely.

You might as well have cried "sir" to a mountain torrent. Richard hurried on, for he was furious.

"You nasty, dirty, dusty dowdy! How dare you come here to disgrace me in my own house and premises, after my sending you L50! To take the very time, too, when—when Richard gasped for breath; and the laugh of his guests rang in his ears, and got into his chest, and choked him. Jane Fairfield drew herself up, and her tears were dried.

"I did not come to disgrace you! I came to see my boy, and—"

"Ha!" interrupted Richard, "to see him."

He turned to Leonard: "You have written to this woman, then?"

"No, sir, I have not."

"I believe you lie."

"He does not lie; and he is as good as yourself, and better, Richard Avenel," exclaimed Mrs. Fairfield; "and I won't stand here and hear him insulted,—that's what I won't. And as for your L50, there are forty- five of it; and I'll work my fingers to the bone till I pay back the other five. And don't be afeard I shall disgrace you, for I'll never look on your face agin; and you're a wicked, bad man,—that's what you are!"

The poor woman's voice was so raised and so shrill, that any other and more remorseful feeling which Richard might have conceived was drowned in his apprehensions that she would be overheard by his servants or his guests,—a masculine apprehension, with which females rarely sympathize; which, on the contrary, they are inclined to consider a mean and cowardly terror on the part of their male oppressors.

"Hush! hold your infernal squall,—do'." said Mr. Avenel, in a tone that he meant to be soothing. "There—sit down—and don't stir till I come back again, and can talk to you calmly. Leonard, follow me, and help to explain things to our guests."

Leonard stood still, but shook his head slightly.

"What do you mean, sir?" said Richard Avenel, in a very portentous growl. "Shaking your head at me? Do you intend to disobey me? You had better take care!"

Leonard's front rose; he drew one arm round his mother, and thus he spoke,

"Sir, you have been kind to me, and generous, and that thought alone silenced my indignation when I heard you address such language to my mother; for I felt that, if I spoke, I should say too much. Now I speak, and it is to say, shortly, that— "

"Hush, boy," said poor Mrs. Fairfield, frightened; "don't mind me. I did not come to make mischief, and ruin your prospex. I'll go!"

"Will you ask her pardon, Mr. Avenel?" said Leonard, firmly; and he advanced towards his uncle.

Richard, naturally hot and intolerant of contradiction, was then excited, not only by the angry emotions, which, it must be owned, a man so mortified, and in the very flush of triumph, might well experience, but by much more wine than he was in the habit of drinking; and when Leonard approached him, he misinterpreted the movement into one of menace and aggression. He lifted his arm: "Come a step nearer," said he, between his teeth, "and I'll knock you down." Leonard advanced the forbidden step; but as Richard caught his eye, there was something in that eye— not defying, not threatening, but bold and dauntless—which Richard recognized and respected, for that something spoke the Freeman. The uncle's arm mechanically fell to his side. "You cannot strike me, Mr. Avenel," said Leonard, "for you are aware that I could not strike again my mother's brother. As her son, I once more say to you,—ask her pardon."

"Ten thousand devils! Are you mad?—or do you want to drive me mad? You insolent beggar, fed and clothed by my charity! Ask her pardon!— what for? That she has made me the object of jeer and ridicule with that d—-d cotton gown and those double-d—-d thick shoes—I vow and protest they've got nails in them! Hark ye, sir, I've been insulted by her, but I'm not to be bullied by you. Come with me instantly, or I discard you; not a shilling of mine shall you have as long as I live. Take your choice: be a peasant, a labourer, or— "

"A base renegade to natural affection, a degraded beggar indeed!" cried Leonard, his breast heaving, and his cheeks in a glow. "Mother, Mother, come away. Never fear,—I have strength and youth, and we will work together as before."

But poor Mrs. Fairfield, overcome by her excitement, had sunk down into Richard's own handsome morocco leather easy-chair, and could neither speak nor stir.

"Confound you both!" muttered Richard. "You can't be seen creeping out of my house now. Keep her here, you young viper, you; keep her till I come back; and then, if you choose to go, go and be— "

Not finishing his sentence, Mr. Avenel hurried out of the room, and locked the door, putting the key into his pocket. He paused for a moment in the hall, in order to collect his thoughts, drew three or four deep breaths, gave himself a great shake, and, resolved to be faithful to his principle of doing one thing at a time, shook off in that shake all disturbing recollection of his mutinous captives. Stern as Achilles when he appeared to the Trojans, Richard Avenel stalked back to his lawn.

CHAPTER XIX.

Brief as had been his absence, the host could see that, in the interval, a great and notable change had come over the spirit of his company. Some of those who lived in the town were evidently preparing to return home on foot; those who lived at a distance, and whose carriages (having been sent away, and ordered to return at a fixed hour) had not yet arrived, were gathered together in small knots and groups; all looked sullen and displeased, and all instinctively turned from their host as he passed them by. They felt they had been lectured, and they were more put out than Richard himself. They did not know if they might not be lectured again. This vulgar man, of what might he not be capable? Richard's shrewd sense comprehended in an instant all the difficulties of his position; but he walked on deliberately and directly towards Mrs. M'Catchley, who was standing near the grand marquee with the Pompleys and the dean's lady. As those personages saw him make thus boldly towards them, there was a flutter. "Hang the fellow!" said the colonel, intrenching himself in his stock, "he is coming here. Low and shocking —what shall we do? Let us stroll on." But Richard threw himself in the way of the retreat. "Mrs. M'Catchley," said he, very gravely, and offering her his arm, "allow me three words with you."

The poor widow looked very much discomposed. Mrs. Pompley pulled her by the sleeve. Richard still stood gazing into her face, with his arm extended. She hesitated a minute, and then took the arm.

"Monstrous impudent!" cried the colonel.

"Let Mrs. M'Catchley alone, my dear," responded Mrs. Pompley; "she will know how to give him a lesson."

"Madam," said Richard, as soon as he and his companion were out of hearing, "I rely on you to do me a favour."

"On me?"

"On you, and you alone. You have influence with all those people, and a word from you will effect what I desire. Mrs. M'Catchley," added Richard, with a solemnity that was actually imposing, "I flatter myself that you have some friendship for me, which is more than I can say of any other soul in these grounds; will you do me this favour, ay or no?"

"What is it, Mr. Avenel?" asked Mrs. M'Catchley, much disturbed, and somewhat softened,—for she was by no means a woman without feeling; indeed, she considered herself nervous.

"Get all your friends—all the company, in short-to come back into the tent for refreshments, for anything. I want to say a few words to them."

"Bless me! Mr. Avenel—a few words!" cried the widow, "but that's just what they're all afraid of. You must pardon me, but you really can't ask people to a /dejeune dansant/, and then—scold 'em!"

"I'm not going to scold them," said Air. Avenel, very seriously,—"upon my honour, I'm not. I'm going to make all right, and I even hope afterwards that the dancing may go on—and that you will honour me again with your hand. I leave you to your task; and believe me, I'm not an ungrateful man." He spoke, and bowed—not without some dignity—and vanished within the breakfast division of the marquee. There he busied himself in re-collecting the waiters, and directing them to re-arrange the mangled remains of the table as they best could. Mrs. M'Catchley, whose curiosity and interest were aroused, executed her commission with all the ability and tact of a woman of the world, and in less than a quarter of an hour the marquee was filled, the corks flew, the champagne bounced and sparkled, people drank in silence, munched fruits and cakes, kept up their courage with the conscious sense of numbers, and felt a great desire to know what was coming. Mr. Avenel, at the head of the table, suddenly rose.

"Ladies and Gentlemen," said he, "I have taken the liberty to invite you once more into this tent, in order to ask you to sympathize with me upon an occasion which took us all a little by surprise today.

"Of course, you all know I am a new man,—the maker of my own fortunes."

A great many heads bowed involuntarily. The words were said manfully, and there was a general feeling of respect. "Probably, too," resumed Mr. Avenel, "you may know that I am the son of very honest tradespeople. I say honest, and they are not ashamed of me; I say tradespeople, and I'm not ashamed of them. My sister married and settled at a distance. I took her son to educate and bring up. But I did not tell her where he was, nor even that I had returned from America; I wished to choose my own time for that, when I could give her the surprise, not only of a rich brother, but of a son whom I intended to make a gentleman, so far as manners and education can make one. Well, the poor dear woman has found me out sooner than I expected, and turned the tables on me by giving me a surprise of her own invention. Pray, forgive the confusion this little family-scene has created; and though I own it was very laughable at the moment, and I was wrong to say otherwise, yet I am sure I don't judge ill of your good hearts, when I ask you to think what brother and sister must feel who parted from each other when they were boy and girl. To me" (and Richard gave a great gulp, for he felt that a great gulp alone could swallow the abominable lie he was about to utter)—"to me this has been a very happy occasion! I'm a plain man: no one can take ill what I've said. And wishing that you may be all as happy in your family as I am in mine—humble though it be—I beg to drink your very good healths!"

There was a universal applause when Richard sat down; and so well in his plain way had he looked the thing, and done the thing, that at least half of those present—who till then had certainly disliked and half despised him—suddenly felt that they were proud of his acquaintance. For however aristocratic this country of ours may be, and however especially aristocratic be the genteeler classes in provincial towns and coteries, there is nothing which English folks, from the highest to the lowest, in their hearts so respect as a man who has risen from nothing, and owns it frankly. Sir Compton Delaval, an old baronet, with a pedigree as long as a Welshman's, who had been reluctantly decoyed to the feast by his three unmarried daughters—not one of whom, however, had hitherto condescended even to bow to the host—now rose. It was his right,—he was the first person there in rank and station.

"Ladies and Gentlemen," quoth Sir Compton Delaval, "I am sure that I express the feelings of all present when I say that we have heard with great delight and admiration the words addressed to us by our excellent host. [Applause.] And if any of us, in what—Mr. Avenel describes justly as the surprise of the moment, were betrayed into an unseemly merriment at—at—[the dean's lady whispered 'some of the']—some of the —some of the—" repeated Sir Compton, puzzled, and coming to a deadlock ["holiest sentiments," whispered the dean's lady]—"ay, some of the holiest sentiments in our nature, I beg him to accept our sincerest apologies. I can only say, for my part, that I am proud to rank Mr. Avenel amongst the gentlemen of the county" (here Sir Compton gave a sounding thump on the table), "and to thank him for one of the most brilliant entertainments it has ever been my lot to witness. If he won his fortune honestly, he knows how to spend it nobly."

Whiz went a fresh bottle of champagne.

"I am not accustomed to public speaking, but I could not repress my sentiments. And I've now only to propose to you the health of our host. Richard Avenel, Esquire; and to couple with that the health of his— very interesting sister, and long life to them both."

The sentence was half drowned in enthusiastic plaudits, and in three cheers for Richard Avenel, Esquire, and his very interesting sister.

"I'm a cursed humbug," thought Richard Avenel, as he wiped his forehead; "but the world is such a humbug!" Then he glanced towards Mrs. M'Catehley and, to his great satisfaction, saw Mrs. M'Catchley with her handkerchief before her eyes.

Truth must be told; although the fair widow might certainly have contemplated the probability of accepting Mr. Avenel as a husband, she had never before felt the least bit in love with him; and now she did. There is something in courage and candour—in a word, in manliness—that all women, the most worldly, do admire in men; and Richard Avenel, humbug though his conscience said he was, seemed to Mrs. M'Catchley like a hero.

The host saw his triumph. "Now for another dance!" said he, gayly; and he was about to offer his hand to Mrs. M'Catchley, when Sir Compton Delaval seizing it, and giving it a hearty shake, cried, "You have not yet danced with my eldest daughter; so if you'll not ask her, why, I must offer her to you as your partner. Here, Sarah."

Miss Sarah Delaval, who was five feet eight, and as stately as she was tall, bowed her head graciously; and Mr. Avenel, before he knew where he was, found her leaning on his arm. But as he passed into the next division of the tent, he had to run the gauntlet of all the gentlemen, who thronged round to shake hands with him. Their warm English hearts could not be satisfied till they had so repaired the sin of their previous haughtiness and mockery. Richard Avenel might then have safely introduced his sister—gown, kerchief, thick shoes, and all—to the crowd; but he had no such thought. He thanked Heaven devoutly that she was safely under lock and key.

It was not till the third dance that he could secure Mrs. M'Catchley's hand, and then it was twilight. The carriages were at the door, but no one yet thought of going. People were really enjoying themselves. Mr. Avenel had had time, in the interim, to mature all his plans for completing and consummating that triumph which his tact and pluck had drawn from his momentary disgrace. Excited as he was with wine, and suppressed passion, he had yet the sense to feel that, when all the halo that now surrounded him had evaporated, and Mrs. M'Catchley was redelivered up to the Pompleys, whom he felt to be the last persons his interest could desire for her advisers, the thought of his low relations would return with calm reflection. Now was the time. The iron was hot, now was the time to strike it, and forge the enduring chain. As he led Mrs. M'Catchley after the dance, into the lawn, he therefore said tenderly,—

"How shall I thank you for the favour you have done me?"

"Oh!" said Mrs. M'Catchley, warmly, "It was no favour, and I am so glad—" She stopped.

"You're not ashamed of me, then, in spite of what has happened?"

"Ashamed of you! Why, I should be so proud of you, if I were—"

"Finish the sentence and say—'your wife!'—there, it is out. My dear madam, I am rich, as you know; I love you very heartily. With your help, I think I can make a figure in a larger world than this: and that, whatever my father, my grandson at least will be—but it is time enough to speak of him. What say you?—you—turn away. I'll not tease you, —it is not my way. I said before, ay or no; and your kindness so emboldens me that I say it again, ay or no?"

"But you take me so unawares—so—so—Lord! my dear Mr. Avenel; you are so hasty—I—I—" And the widow actually blushed, and was genuinely bashful.

"Those horrid Pompleys!" thought Richard, as he saw the colonel bustling up with Mrs. M'Catchley's cloak on his arm. "I press for your answer," continued the suitor, speaking very fast. "I shall leave this place to- morrow, if you will not give it."

"Leave this place—leave me?"

"Then you will be mine?"

"Ah, Mr. Avenel!" said the widow, languidly, and leaving her hand in his, "who can resist you?"

Up came Colonel Pompley; Richard took the shawl: "No hurry for that now,
Colonel,—Mrs. M'Catchley feels already at home here."

Ten minutes afterwards, Richard Avenel so contrived that it was known by the whole company that their host was accepted by the Honourable Mrs. M'Catchley. And every one said, "He is a very clever man and a very good fellow," except the Pompleys—and the Pompleys were frantic. Mr. Richard Avenel had forced his way into the aristocracy of the country; the husband of an Honourable, connected with peers!

"He will stand for our city—Vulgarian!" cried the colonel. "And his wife will walk out before me," cried the colonel's lady,—"nasty woman!" And she burst into tears.

The guests were gone; and Richard had now leisure to consider what course to pursue with regard to his sister and her son.

His victory over his guests had in much softened his heart towards his relations; but he still felt bitterly aggrieved at Mrs. Fairfield's unseasonable intrusion, and his pride was greatly chafed by the boldness of Leonard. He had no idea of any man whom he had served, or meant to serve, having a will of his own, having a single thought in opposition to his pleasure. He began, too, to feel that words had passed between him and Leonard which could not be well forgotten by either, and would render their close connection less pleasant than heretofore. He, the great Richard Avenel, beg pardon of Mrs. Fairfield, the washerwoman! No; she and Leonard must beg his. "That must be the first step," said Richard Avenel; "and I suppose they have come to their senses." With that expectation, he unlocked the door of his parlour, and found himself in complete solitude. The moon, lately risen, shone full into the room, and lit up every corner. He stared round bewildered,—the birds had flown. "Did they go through the keyhole?" said Air. Avenel. "Ha! I see! the window is open!" The window reached to the ground. Mr. Avenel, in his excitement, had forgotten that easy mode of egress. "Well," said he, throwing himself into his easy-chair, "I suppose I shall soon hear from them: they'll be wanting my money fast enough, I fancy." His eye caught sight of a letter, unsealed, lying on the table. He opened it, and saw bank-notes to the amount of L50,—the widow's forty-five country notes, and a new note, Bank of England, that he had lately given to Leonard. With the money were these lines, written in Leonard's bold, clear writing, though a word or two here and there showed that the hand had trembled,—

> I thank you for all you have done to one whom you regarded as the object of charity. My mother and I forgive what has passed. I depart with her. You bade me make my choice, and I have made it.

LEONARD FAIRFIELD.

The paper dropped from Richard's hand, and he remained mute and remorseful for a moment. He soon felt, however, that he had no help for it but working himself up into a rage. "Of all people in the world," cried Richard, stamping his foot on the floor, "there are none so disagreeable, insolent, and ungrateful as poor relations. I wash my hands of them!"